The Kiss

Volume 2

More Meanings of a Kiss

Richard Lindstrom, PhD.

ISBN: 9798343448993
Imprint: Independently published

Table of Contents

A KISS OF CHOICE

***

The first time that Alice met Kyle she knew he was one of a kind. Sure, he was handsome. He carried himself well. He wasn't like the other men she had known. In many ways, Alice felt like Kyle was out-of-place, perhaps ahead of his time in a lot of ways, when they crossed paths back on that hot summer day in 1987, a moment in time she would never forget.

Alice walked into the bar with her friend, Ginger, the two of them having been stood up by their dates that Friday evening. After hours of getting dolled-up and making sure their wardrobe was free of wrinkles, they felt the need to commiserate with one another by heading to the

Irish-themed pub across the street, McKinley's, and enjoying a few shots and a pair of pints. As Alice entered, she was still stewing over the fact that Robbie had stood her up and swearing off men entirely as she adjusted the strap of her purse on her shoulder. It was when her attention was caught by a tall and strapping gentleman staring intensely at the news screen toward the back of the bar, that all notions of swearing of men entirely became negotiable.

"*Alice*," Ginger said as she nudged her in the ribs. "Stop staring! He'll see you."

The gentleman, as though it were on cue, averted his attention from the television and glanced at Alice. She looked away, her heart thumping like the beat of an up-tempo percussion number as she walked over to a table with Ginger and sat down. Back facing the gentleman, Alice said, "You don't think he saw me looking, did you?"

Ginger took a quick glimmer at the man over Alice's shoulder. "I think so, yeah."

Alice closed her eyes, "Crap."

"Just go over and talk to him."

Alice shook her head, "No! Are you kidding me?" She batted the comment aside with a swipe of her hand. "Besides, tonight is supposed to be girl's night. I thought we were swearing off men entirely after not one, but *two* men stood us up."

Ginger smirked, "I say a lot of things." She jutted her chin, "Besides, that guy is looking at you right now."

A lump formed in Alice's throat. Her eyes went wide, "He is?"

With a nod, Ginger affirmed, "He is."

Alice took a quick glimmer over her shoulder. The man looked away. She did the same. The proverbial cosmic connection which occurred when one person felt a connection kindling with the other was happening.

What harm is there in just saying hi? Alice told herself. Even if he was a creep, even if he turned out to be just like all the other men Alice had met (save her father, brother, and grandfather), she was certain she could squeeze a free drink out of the ordeal, one of the many reparations women rightfully took advantage of in a world dominated by men.

"*Go*," Ginger insisted as she tapped Alice's foot with her own. "Just say hi. Ask him how he's doing?"

Alice laughed, "Ask him how he's doing? Smooth, Ginger."

"Whatever," Ginger said. "Up to you. I say go for it. If he's a jerk, just make sure you put in your order for a Tequila Sunrise first."

Nerves spiking, Alice gritted her teeth, drew a breath, composed herself, and headed toward the bar. She tossed her hair, hoping the gentleman she spotted would take notice, which he did. She came alongside him at the bar. Flagged down the bartender. Put in her order for one Tequila Sunrise and saw the gentleman was still very much glued to the news report on the television. From what Alice could make out, the report was covering some kind of explosion near downtown.

Just talk, Alice told herself. *Say something!* She cleared her throat. Pointed to the television. Glanced at the gentleman fervently glued to the television, and said, "What's that all about?" Alice wanted to roll her eyes. *Nice way to start a conversation*, her mind chirped.

The gentleman turned his head toward Alice. For a moment, she thought she might faint. He was even more handsome up close than he was from a distance: raven-colored hair. Steel blue eyes. The subtlest of dimples. A stylish five-o-clock shadow that Alice wanted to trace a finger across.

The gentleman said nothing. He looked at Alice quizzically. Appraising his eyes, Alice saw there was a kind of rusted patina to them indicative of a man who saw perhaps more than he wanted to in his lifetime.

"I'm sorry?" the gentleman apologized.

Alice blinked several times before mustering the courage to speak. "Oh," she gestured to the television, "I'm sorry. I was asking what that was all about, that story on the television there."

The gentleman forced a smile, "Oh, right, something about a gas leak, an explosion, I think."

Eyes pinned to the television; Alice watched as dozens of emergency vehicles flooded the scene - a seemingly abandoned warehouse where smoke plumed out of a crater-sized hole in the roof.

"How weird," Alice said. "I wonder what happened."

The gentleman, patting down his wardrobe—which, to Alice, looked as though it had been all purchased recently even down to his shoes—asked Alice what time it was.

Alice glanced at the Mikey Mouse watched her father gifted her on her wrist, "Eight-o-six."

The gentleman nodded, "And the day? What day is it?"

A smirk formed on Alice's lips. *Maybe he's had one too many*, she figured, "Friday," gesturing to the calendar behind the register that read MARCH, 1986, "All day."

"Oh," the gentleman affirmed. "Right."

Something about the way his hair was parted sparked curiosity in Alice. Everything about his style and the way he carried himself seemed so different than the other men she had known.

"What's your name?" Alice asked.

The question seemed to spark fear in the gentleman. He was fidgety, a bit on edge, "You want to know my name?" he asked.

Alice blushed, "You don't have to tell me if you don't want to."

The gentleman paused for a moment. To Alice, he seemed to be weighing his options in the way that his eyes flickered. "Kyle," he said. "My name is Kyle."

Extending her petite hand, Alice said, "Pleasure to meet you, Kyle. My name is Alice."

Kyle molded his palm around Alice's and shook. His hand felt calloused, indicative of a man who engaged in rigorous physical activity on a regular basis, which was already apparent based on his tall and athletic frame.

"So," Alice said, "um…" *Think! Say something!* "What do you do for a living?"

Kyle bit his lip and squinted, "It's hard to explain." He held up his hand. He seemed to be relaxing a little. He wasn't slumping his shoulders as much. His tone was a bit less apprehensive. "I know that sounds like an excuse, but…"

"*Hmm*," Alice said as she slipped down on the seat beside him. "Sounds intriguing. Are you a spy?"

Kyle laughed, "No, I'm not a spy. I, uh," he lowered his voice to a hush, "I do work for the government, though. But it's not as appealing or alluring as it sounds. Trust me."

"Do you travel a lot?"

The question made Kyle huff, "Yeah," he said with a sigh. "A little bit." He threw a look over his shoulder toward the back door leading out.

Alice asked, "Are you waiting for someone?"

Kyle shook his head. "No, it's just."

He doesn't want to talk to you, Alice told herself. *Just leave him be.* "I'm sorry," she offered. "I know that I just walked up here and interrupted your evening. I can go."

"It's not that," Kyle answered. "It's just." He squinted. "It's hard to explain. I get worried about pretty women walking up to me and striking up a conversation."

Alice blushed, "Why is that?"

"Because of my work. Like I said, I travel a lot and it tends to be cumbersome on a relationship."

"I never said anything about starting a relationship. I was just hoping to have a drink with you."

"With me?"

Alice bit her lip, "Yes. With you."

"Why me?" Kyle inquired.

"Because you're…well, handsome. You have a certain look about you. Mysterious, maybe."

Kyle smirked, "It's not my intention to come off that way."

Alice asked, "Are you one of those, how do I phrase it, *lone wolf* types?"

"In a way," Kyle said. "But I very much enjoy the company of others. Like I said, my work keeps me moving a lot. It's put strain on the relationships I've had before. I just don't want to get anyone's hopes up, is all."

Something about Kyle was just too appealing for Alice to dismiss. It was difficult for her to articulate why she couldn't just break free of him. Even though he was cryptic in his replies, she still wanted to know more.

"I'll tell you what," Alice said. "How about I buy you a drink? After we finish our drinks, if the conversation feels like it isn't going anywhere, if you or I think it's a waste of time, we can shake hands, part ways, and go about our night."

A perplexed look radiated across Kyle's face. "You're very persistent," he said with an intrigued timbre, "Aren't you?"

Alice, glancing at Ginger, saw her wink and give her a small gesture. Alice knew Ginger long enough by now that the gesture meant: *Keep going!*

"What do you say?" Alice asked. "Can I buy you a drink?"

A moment passed as Kyle locked eyes with Alice. Alice felt her chest flutter as both of them smiled. When the moment passed, Kyle flagged down the bartender and asked him for two finger's worth of whiskey. By the time the drink was finished, Alice and Kyle felt inclined to order another, and one more after that. Once the bill had been paid, the two of them felt inclined to make a date to see each other again.

***

1988

Alice giggled louder than she ever had in her life as Kyle used his fingers to tickle her belly. They rolled around on the bed, laughing and taunting each other playfully as they spent the early hours of a Saturday morning making love and putting off getting out of bed as long as possible. It had been almost a year since they first met in the bar, and there were no signs the honeymoon phase was waning.

Alice, lying on her side, cupped Kyle's face in her hands, "So much for traveling."

A pensive expression overcame Kyle, "What do you mean?"

"When we first met," Alice intoned, "You said you travelled a lot for work. You said something about relationships suffering because of how often you had to leave." She shrugged, "I haven't seen you do anything but take meetings with those men in suits every once in a while."

Kyle sighed, "They haven't called me up to travel yet, but I'm sure it's coming soon though."

Alice was more than familiar by now at the secretive nature of Kyle's job. He wasn't allowed to say what he did or introduce her to those men in suits who occasionally stopped by to say hello. They never shook hands with Alice, never said a word to her, never made eye contact with her. If anything, they appeared somewhat perturbed at the fact that Kyle was in a relationship with her. When Alice asked Kyle about this, he simply kissed her on the forehead—which he always did at least once a day—and told her not to worry.

"Where *do* you go?" Alice asked, "When you have to travel, I mean?"

Kyle shook his head. He took a finger and ran it down the bridge of Alice's nose. "I can't tell you that," he murmured, "We've talked about this."

"I just wish I knew more, is all. I wish I knew what you did for a living. I'd be lying if I didn't say I wasn't, well, *titillated* by the mystery of it all."

"Again, my love," Kyle answered, "it's not as thrilling as you may think."

A wry smile formed on Alice's lips, "I doubt that. I know you well enough by now that I just think you're telling me what I want to hear."

Kyle held Alice's face in-between his hands, "You love me, right?"

She nodded.

"You trust me, yes?"

She nodded again.

Kyle planted a delicate kiss on her cheek, "Then let's just roll with that, unless you have any objections, that is?"

The warmest of grins spread from one of Alice's ears to the next. She trusted Kyle. He never gave her any reasons not to. He was always present, though it took him some effort at the start of the relationship to fully open up to her. He was guarded, a bit scared, perhaps. But once Kyle had given himself over to Alice, she was never disappointed for a minute. Sure, they were two human beings who occasionally butted heads with one another— but the love they shared always brought them back to level footing.

That night, they opted for takeout. The Oscars were on television. Kyle never seemed to be interested in watching anything. They went to movies once in a while, caught up on television shows and stayed up to date on world events. But there was always something in Kyle's eyes when they did these things. He looked bored, a bit irritated. Nevertheless, he still kept his arm around Alice and occasionally whispered in her ear, "I love you." By the time the Best Actor category was announced on the television, Alice turned to Kyle and asked him for his prediction.

"Michael Douglas," Kyle said without thinking twice.

The envelope was ripped open. The winner was announced. Sure enough, it was Michael Douglas who went home with the Oscar.

***

The two of them decided to name their first child Adam. Alice, holding the bundle of joy in her arms, felt it was a more than fitting name as Kyle, seated on the hospital bed with his arm around his wife, smiled and said nothing as the two of them looked lovingly at their son.

"He looks like you," Alice said. "No question about it."

Kyle laughed, "How can you tell? All babies look the same."

"But this one is ours," Alice kissed the top of Adam's head.

A knock sounded on the door. Alice and Kyle turned their heads to see one of the men in suits Kyle worked with standing in the doorway. His face was placid. He looked, as he always did, emotionless as he gestured for

Kyle to join him outside. Of all the days Alice did not want

Kyle to discuss anything work-related, today was that day.

"*Kyle,*" Alice whispered in protest.

Kyle, standing, told Alice he would only be a

moment as he followed the man outside. He closed the door

behind him as Kyle and the man in the suit discussed

something that caused a frown to become etched into

Kyle's face.

Alice, perturbed, watched the muted conversation

play out for a few minutes. Once it ended, Kyle came back

into the room and looked at her with a dismayed

expression. He took a glance at the man in the suit waiting

for him in the hallway as he repeatedly checked his watch.

"What is it?" Alice asked.

"I have to go," Kyle said. "I have to go on a trip."

The words felt like sharp pin pricks in Alice's soul.

It had been three years since she met Kyle, one since she

married him. In that entire time, he had never been called away from home. She always knew the moment was on the horizon, waiting to rear its head. She just never thought in a million years it would happen during the birth of their son.

"No," Alice said. "You can't go. Not now. You can't be serious."

Kyle held up his hand, "I have no choice, honey. I *have* to go. I'm obligated."

Anger welled up inside of Alice, "You have an obligation to stay with your wife, with your son."

"I know," Kyle answered, "But this has to be done. I'll be back before you know it."

"When?"

"Tonight. No later than 5 p.m."

"Oh," Alice remarked, thinking that Kyle would have been gone for days, if not weeks. "Why so quickly?"

"It's always that quick," Kyle answered. "And when I get back, I'll be…well, tired. I'll need a moment to recoup. But I'll be back at 5 p.m. sharp. No earlier, no later."

It was a compromise Alice was willing to make. Sure, she did not want Kyle to leave at all, but such a brief amount of time gone was something with which she was willing to comply. In three years, Kyle had never been pulled away for work. She loved him. She supported him. He would be back in less than eight hours, according to the time the clock on the wall inside the hospital room read.

Kyle kissed his son, then his wife. He went outside to join the man in the suit who handed him a file before the two disappeared from sight. As promised, Kyle returned later that evening. As promised, he walked through the door of the hospital room at exactly 5 p.m. As promised, he looked tired, but well above what Alice had expected.

When 5 p.m. hit, Alice awoke to find Kyle standing in the doorway leading into her hospital room. His clothes were tattered. His hair was a mess. A scratch crusted with blood ran down from his left eyebrow to the top part of his lip. He was panting. Sweating. His eyes were wide and manic.

"*Kyle!*" Alice said as she sat up in her bed. "My God! What happened to you?"

Kyle held up his hand, "Just stay right there. I can't touch you."

"Why not?"

Kyle sighed, "It's a long story."

Little Adam squeaked from the plastic cradle beside Alice's bed. She picked him up, cooing to the child as Kyle slipped down into the chair in the corner of the room with a groan. He looked taxed, still attempting to catch his breath like he had just run a marathon.

Alice stared daggers at Kyle. "Tell me what's going on," she requested.

Kyle shook his head, "I can't."

Appraising his wardrobe and disheveled appearance, "It would be in your best interest if you did."

Kyle cocked his head to the side, "I'm not in the mood, Alice."

"I just gave birth to a child this morning," Alice huffed. "Whatever physical endurance you clearly just put yourself through *pales* in comparison."

Hands held up in submission, Kyle said, "You know what my job entails."

"I know it entails secrecy," Alice answered. "And I was on board with that for a while." She jutted her chin toward the door, "I've put up with these mystery men stopping by our house, glaring at me, and exchanging secrets with you for the past three years. But enough is enough. You can't come in here looking like you just tuned up someone for the mob and tell me not to ask questions."

"Alice—"

Alice held up a finger, "You're going to tell me what's going on. If you don't, then I'll just press those men in those nifty little suits that stop by on occasion and ask them. Maybe they'll tell me."

The threat caused the whites of Kyle's eyes to show. He stood up. Crooked a finger at his wife. "Alice," he said gravely, "you can never, and I mean *never* speak to those men. You don't understand—"

"I *don't*!" Alice grumbled. "All I know is that my husband just walked into a hospital room on the day of his son's birth looking like he just went through hell. I deserve to know. I'm not going to stay in the dark any longer. Tell me, Kyle. Tell me what the hell it is that you're involved in."

The look on Kyle's face was one of sheer defeat. He ran his hand through his hair, wincing and then grabbing his shoulder.

"Are you okay?" Alice asked, still maddened but concerned for the health of her husband.

Kyle nodded, "Just a few welts and bruises. Nothing that can't heal with time and Tylenol."

"Kyle," Alice whispered, relaxing a bit more and trying to reason with her spouse, "I love you. I'll support you. But you have to give me something, anything to help me understand."

Kyle approached Alice's bedside. He stooped down on one knee. He took her hand into his and rallied a moment before speaking. Alice couldn't help but note that his beard appeared a bit longer than it did earlier that morning.

"My work is dangerous," Kyle explained. "But I don't kill people, I don't hurt people if that's what you're wondering. When I said that I travel for work occasionally, it's true. But..." he sighed, "I lied when I said I work for the government."

The muscles in Alice's jaw tensed. It was the first time Kyle had indicated he was being dishonest his entire life.

"So," Alice said, "who *do* you work for?"

"A private organization," Kyle said. "They have contracts with the government. Defense technology, putting it simply. I work on helping them, well, calibrate their equipment."

"What kind of equipment?"

He shook his head, "I can't tell you that. What I can tell you is that what happened today was a fluke. An error was made. No one was hurt, thankfully."

"*You* were hurt," Alice said with a bit of scorn.

Kyle nodded, "I know. But it won't happen again. I promise you."

Alice shook her head, wanting to believe her husband but having a hard time doing so.

"Honey," Kyle encouraged, "I need you to trust me. This won't happen again. I swear."

Sincerity coated Kyle's words. He looked at his wife for a long moment before she nodded, kissed him on the hand, and told her husband she just wanted to forget what happened and focus on the new life she had brought into the world. The matter was never brought up again. Kyle was better about keeping her in the loop on his travels. He went on two more trips in the following three years. As promised, he returned unscathed, but each time he departed for his brief departures, he seemed a bit more jaded than he had before he left.

***

1998

No trips had been taken in four years. Adam, a young man who was tall enough to reach past his mother's waist, asked his father as they meandered through the zoo if he could purchase a churro. Kyle handed Adam five dollars and told him to hurry back before he set about fetching a seat at a bench in front of the flamingo enclosure with Alice.

Alice looked at her husband. Streaks of grey were in his hair. He was only a man of forty-two-years of age, but he looked as though he was ten years older.

"This is a good day," Alice said. "I'm glad we did this."

Adam nodded. "It is," he said. "I wanted to mark the occasion."

The lines in Alice's brow furrowed, "What occasion?"

Kyle smiled and looked at his wife. "I'm retiring," he said. "Full pension. It's over. No more trips. No more meeting with the men in black suits. I can do whatever I want now."

The reveal made Alice feel as though a weight had been lifted off her shoulders. She closed her eyes and hugged her husband tightly.

"I'd be lying," Alice said, "if I wasn't glad to hear it. This job, whatever it was, took a toll on you."

Kyle nodded. "It did," he said, a palpable history reflected in his tone.

"I just can't believe they cut you loose."

Kyle shook his head, "They didn't." He looked at his wife and kissed her on the cheek, "I chose to."

Alice said, "You just…quit?"

Kyle nodded, "I did. But it won't affect the pension I'm getting. I meant it when I said I could retire."

His wife wanted to know more. She wanted to know about what he did, where he went, why he showed up to the hospital room on the day of Adam's birth looking as though he had gotten into a fight.

"Kyle," Alice said, "what *did* you do for those people?"

"It's hard to explain," Kyle answered. "But that's why I wanted to bring you here. I thought it would be better to, well, *show* you." He pointed toward the flamingo enclosure.

Alice turned her attention to a family near the churro stand: a mother, a father, a son not much older than Adam. They were speaking to Adam, Adam was pointing to Alice and Kyle in reply.

"I'm confused," Alice replied.

"Look at the boy," Kyle said. "The son with that family."

Alice took in the young boy speaking to Adam. He was the same height as Adam. Toted the same smile. Carried himself in a way that Adam did, which was a lot like his father. After a moment, Adam rushed back to his parents with the son in tow. The closer the son came into view, the more Alice felt as though she had met the young man before.

"Mom!" Adam said. "Dad! This is my new friend."

The young boy waved. "Hi," he said. "I'm Kyle."

Alice's heart was racing. She looked at her husband and back to the young boy who said his name was Kyle. In that moment, everything fell into place. Even though she only had a few pieces of the puzzle to work with over the years, Alice understood who the little boy was and exactly why Kyle had requested they go to the zoo. *They're the same person*, Alice thought as she looked into the little boy's eyes. *That's…that's my husband! And he's only a child!*

The young boy's parents came over. The father seemed intrigued as he shook Kyle's hand. "I think we've met before," the father said. "You look familiar to me."

Kyle smiled. "Same," he answered.

The family conversed for a few moments before going their separate ways. Kyle, Alice, and Adam approached the gorilla exhibit, Alice mustering up the courage to say to Kyle: "Was that…was that…*you*? Was that little boy you?"

Kyle nodded. "Yes."

"So," Alice said, still trying to wrap her head around the revelation, "these trips you took. You travelled through—"

Kyle held up a hand. "It's over, now," he said. "Like I said, I made a choice to walk away. You know everything now. I just want you to be willing to make the choice to leave this, well, in the past."

So many questions lingered in Alice's mind—but now she knew the truth. Abiding by her husband's wishes, she nodded, made her choice, and rested her head on Kyle's shoulder. The matter was never discussed again.

When the day ended, Alice caught a glimpse of the little boy named Kyle in the parking lot as they made their way back to the car. The little boy looked at her curiously. He waved. She waved back. She stuck to her choice of not saying a word on the manner again as she gave Kyle one more kiss on the cheek.

A KISS OF EXCITEMENT

***

The bank alarm rang out. Denny fired two shots into the roof. The customers sprawled out on the polished marble floors hollered, fragments of plaster from the ceiling raining down on their heads. Their collective shrieks triggered Rachel's laughter as she slung the bag of cash over her shoulder, grabbed Denny by the hand, and hotfooted it out the front of the bank.

"We did it, baby!" Rachel screamed.

Denny smirked. No matter how many times he looked at Rachel, he couldn't come to terms with how strikingly attractive she was: her petite yet busty frame. The alluring technique in how she tossed her flaxen-colored hair. The million-dollar smile that thawed his otherwise icy temperament since the day they met in the bar just four weeks prior. Denny lived for Rachel. He'd die for her, too.

"Come on," Denny said, pulling Rachel toward the sedan they hotwired for the job. "Cops will be here in a few minutes."

Rachel tossed the bag in the back seat and turned on the radio, "We need some music, baby."

Denny shuffled behind the wheel and cranked the ignition. He knew music would flag down the cops. Hell, someone in the bank was probably on the line with the operator giving a description of their vehicle. Vegas odds were high that the law would catch up them in a flash, but he didn't care. Whatever Rachel want, he would give her. It didn't matter the request no matter how big or small. Denny *lived* for Rachel. He'd die for her, too.

It took just a moment of combing through the airwaves before Rachel landed on "Let Your Love Flow" by The Bellamy Brothers. She chalked it up to fate that she landed on the country hit. Her mother—God rest her— treasured that particular melody. Countless times as a child Rachel had padded her way downstairs, the smell of bacon and eggs lingering in the air, the crack and sizzle of the pan competing with the sounds of the Bellamy Brothers, her mother singing softly along with the music. Before Rachel's old man—may he burn in hell—had drunkenly tossed her down a flight of stairs and cut her life short, Rachel and her mother were attached at the hip. Inseparable. Rachel never loved anyone as intensely as she did her mother—until she met Denny. She lived for Denny. She'd die for him, too.

Denny cranked the ignition and revved the engine. The two lovers locked gazes, their temperatures rising, Rachel cupping Denny's face in her hands and pressing her lips firmly against his. Whenever the two embraced, caressed, or made love, it was, for lack of a better word, exciting.

"Let's hit it," Rachel said.

"Where we headed?" Denny asked.

Her eyes scanned the road outside the windshield. The open highway was ahead of them, flanked on all sides by towering pines. How far they would get was up to God, or fate, or whatever one wanted to call it. Based on the sound of the incoming sirens approaching from a short distance away, it wouldn't be long.

"Doesn't matter," Rachel said. "Just drive, darling."

Denny stamped his foot into the accelerator. The car jolted forward, Denny hollering at the top of his lungs as Rachel turned the volume up on the radio to his maximum setting.

***

Mike Harlow never wanted to be a cop. When he was younger, he wanted to be an astronaut. He was six when he was stopped in front of the television in his father's study, his nose a few inches away from brushing up against the screen. Young Mike observed with innocent admiration as the Challenger shuttle ascended toward the heavens, envisioning himself in the cockpit alongside the other crew members who were boldly going where, well, more than a handful of people had gone before.

"Go! Go! Go!" little Mike whispered, the cheers from the spectators contending with the television reporter updating the viewer on the progress of the shuttle's climb. *One day*, he told himself. *One day, I'll be just like them.*

But when the shuttle burst into flames, Mike, too young to process what was happening until his father explained it to him, the prospect of him being eviscerated into a million little pieces put his aspirations asleep quicker than a narcoleptic on a high dose of melatonin. So, Mike shifted his passions to becoming an archeologist. When he came to the understanding that the life was nothing like Indiana Jones, he opted for chasing a position as a wide receiver for the Broncos. Upon folding his knee back ninety degrees the wrong way his sophomore year of college, he pivoted to a life of finance. Two years of rubbing shoulders with Wall Street yuppies in the Big Apple tainted that option. Mike, never one for booze or vices, had a bad taste in his mouth after witnessing a gaggle of fools addicted to nose candy or Adderall. So, he went back home. He figured he could start up his own business with the classes he took at NYU. Then he met Darlene. Then she got pregnant. The circumstances forced Mike to find something steady and led him to not batting an eye when Darlene's father, the Sheriff, offered him a position as one of his deputies.

Mike never wanted to be a cop—but he found he didn't hate it as much as he thought he would. It was alright. Most of the time was spent chasing down speeders or hauling out drunks who overstayed their welcome in the local watering holes. He was home for dinner almost every night. When Cassie was born, Mike found fulfilment. He loved his wife. He adored his child. His life, though it didn't pan out the way he thought it would when he was a child, ended up faring more than well, so every day that Mike awoke and pinned his badge to his shirt, he smiled.

The cell phone in the cup holder of Mike's cruiser rang. The caller ID, a picture of Darlene holding infant Cassie in her arm, flashed on the screen. The same smirk he put on display every time Mike walked into the house was on his face as he answered the call.

"Hey, hon," he greeted.

"Hey, you," Darlene said. "How's it going?"

Mike, his cruiser idling on the side of the highway, shrugged as he scanned the empty roads. "Not much is happening," he answered. "Your old man's got me on highway detail today."

She asked, "Is he mad at you or something?"

Mike shook his head, "It's that old crap knee of mine. It's been flaring up again."

"Think it'll get in the way of you picking up some steaks tonight for dinner?"

Smiling, Mike replied, "Not a chance."

"Good," his wife answered. "I thought we could have a date night tonight."

The lines in Mike's brow wrinkled, "What's the occasion?"

"The occasion is that I love you."

"Always a good reason."

"Rib eyes," Darlene instructed. "Two of them. I'm taking Cassie next door to Sarah's so we can have a night to ourselves. Make sure you're home by six."

"Well," Mike intoned, "that's up to your father."

Laughing, "Tell him his baby girl said so."

Mike opened his mouth to reply—but then the radio next to him crackled to life: "Mike! Mike, come in!"

"I gotta go, doll," Mike offered, "Someone's getting all hot and bothered over the radio."

"Be safe," she told him.

"I will," he promised.

The dispatcher continued to call Mike's name. He rolled his eyes as he scooped up the transmitter and keyed the button.

"*Easy*," Mike said into the radio. "What's got you all worked up?"

"Bank robbery," the dispatcher said. "Two suspects. A man and a woman. They just shot a bank manager in the leg and took off with a bag of cash. They're headed your way!"

Mike fixed his gaze to the rear-view mirror. Before the dispatcher could finish giving her description, he saw it – a sedan careening down the road straight in his direction. He didn't have enough time to register how fast it was going. The headlamps were flashing, the car horn and the music inside the car was blasting. Eyes wide, Mike palmed the lights and the sirens. The sedan zipped past him, two flashes and the register of gunshots cracking the through the air. The bullets drilled their way into the cruiser's windshield, the rounds missing Mike by inches as he ducked below the wheel.

"Mike!" the dispatcher called out, "You okay?"

Mike keyed the radio with a trembling hand, "Shots fired!"

"Are you okay?"

"I'm fine." Mike shifted the car into drive, "I'm in pursuit."

Mike never wanted to be a cop. He never wanted to end up being shot at and he never had, until that very moment. He felt fearful, vying to be back in his wife's arms and doing nothing more than eating a steak and watching some trash TV. He never wanted to be a cop—but right now, he had to do it.

***

Denny laughed manically as Rachel volleyed two rounds into the cop's windshield. "*Pig!*" he yelled. "I hope those bullets tore through the vest he's wearing."

Rachel reached over and stroked her lover's leg. Denny may have been diagnosed with various different psychological disorders when he was young, in-and-out of institutions his entire life, but she didn't care. She loved him to the ends of the earth. Being around him was a thrill. Plus, her baby doll had never experienced loved before. His whore of a mother had shacked up with too many men to pinpoint who Denny's real father was. Rumor was a cop had knocked her up when she was hauled in for turning tricks on the street. The trade was simple: put out or be locked up. At least that was the story the nuns and the orphanage had told Denny when they weren't beating him with rulers or poking fun at him for being short. Took all of five years of torment before Denny finally whacked one across Sister Theresa's mouth and ran as far away from the place as he could. Denny never had a permanent home after. He drifted from one couch to the next, from one friend to the next, knocking over liquor stores and engaging in petty thievery that garnered him a rap sheet longer than Route 66.

The way Rachel saw it, he was a survivor, a guy who didn't take no flak from anyone. The day they met in the bar, the moment she looked deeply into his steel-blue eyes, she knew who Denny was. She loved him right away. She felt no remorse or fear or apprehension when Denny walked onto the dance floor, clocked the guy that Rachel was dancing with, took her by the arm, and said, "You're mine." She loved it. It turned her on. The moment they left the building, the second they knocked over a diner, stole a car, and decided to rob a bank, she found the man she wanted to spend the rest of her life with, no matter how short it would be.

The cruiser that Rachel shot up was gaining traction. Eyeing the speedometer, Rachel clocked they were closing in at 90-miles-per-hour. She squinted, glancing over her shoulder as the cruiser flashed its headlamps and the cop behind the wheel shouted, "Pull over!" across his loudspeaker.

Denny nudged his gal. "Hey, baby?" he said in that oh-so-sweet tone that made Rachel go weak at the knees. "Put another round into that bastard of a cop, will ya?"

Rachel clutched the gun in her hands and moved toward the window. "You don't even have to ask twice, baby doll," she cooed as she stuck her body partway out of the car and took aim.

***

The whites of Mike's eyes were showing. He saw a pretty young lady, a cannon of a firearm in her hand. She stuck her body halfway out of the car, laughing as she took aim at Mike's windshield.

"Shit!" Mike blurted, wrenching the wheel to the left and turning out of the line of fire.

Three gunshots splintered the windshield, one of the rounds nearly clipping Mike in the shoulder as the cruiser fishtailed and struggled to gain traction. Part of him thought he should throw in the towel. If one of the bullets hit their target, Darlene would be crying over his open casket before the week was out. Cassie would be without a father. God only knows what life for the two of them would look like if he were buried six feet under the earth. He had faith that Darlene would make it work, mourning him properly them moving on with her life and carving out a good life for Cassie. Heck, he'd even want her to find another man, to be happy and live a fulfilled life. Yet, the hypothetical nature of it all was something in which he didn't want to indulge. On the other hand, the two crazed lunatics he was pursuing were clearly unhinged, firing blindly at anyone and anything like some kind of modern-day Bonnie and Clyde. Someone was bound to get caught in the crossfire, some innocent bystander who would end up getting run down by their car, an old woman or—God forbid—even a kid. Good heavens, based on the way the woman was callously firing off her gun, one of the bullets might stray, go through a window of a nearby home, and kill some kid playing with his toys in his bedroom.

It's your job, Mike reminded himself. *You may not have wanted it, but it's what you agreed to do. You're the only thing standing in their way. Stop them before they do something unthinkable.*

The woman discharging the gun ran out of rounds. As she crawled back into the car, Mike was close enough to see the two of them laughing as the sedan bobbed from left to right and back again.

Mike scooped up his radio, "It's Harlow, I need some backup. Where are the closest units?"

The dispatcher replied, "Six miles out. They're catching up, but it's going to take a minute."

Mike knew that anything could happen in six miles. Someone was bound to get hurt. If it had to be someone, he'd prefer it was him. He'd do what he could to stay alive, to make sure he made it to the grocery store and fulfilled the plans Darlene had for them to share an intimate evening together. But he knew it was up to God. All he could do was be an instrument of His justice.

He gripped the steering wheel, his eyes focused on the rear-end of the sedan as he mashed down on the gas pedal and prepared to ram the vehicle as hard as he possibly could. Mike closed the distance, gritted his teeth, and prepared for impact as the sedan sped down the stretch of pine-laced highway.

***

The cruiser slammed into the back of the sedan. Denny and Rachel felt the jolt and were thrown forward, the two of them bracing as the car wobbled from side to side.

"*Damn it!*" Denny cursed, eyeing the rear-view mirror as the cruiser prepared to close in for another tap. "That damn cop just won't let up." He glanced at Rachel, "Shoot him again, baby!"

Rachel held up her firearm, the slide racked back to empty, "I'm out, honey."

Danny retrieved the gun from under his seat and slapped it into his lover's hand. "Here," he ordered, "Split open his head like a cantaloupe."

The request caused a giggle to trickle out of Rachel's mouth, "I'll make you proud, Denny darling."

Denny leaned over and kissed Rachel on the cheek. She chambered a round into the weapon and prepared to

lean out of the car once again—but when the cruiser
slammed into the back of the sedan, the gun was knocked
from her grip. The weapon fell to the floormat, Rachel
cursing as she leaned over and fumbled around.

"Come on!" Denny screamed. "What the heck are
you doing?"

"I'm trying, baby!" Rachel cried. "Damn cop made
me drop the gun."

Denny reached over and squeezed Rachel's arm,
pain searing through her skin and tendons and causing her
to wince.

"He didn't *make* you do anything," Denny growled.
"Pick that damn thing up and put that pig in the ground.
I'm not going to tell you twice."

The last thing Rachel ever wanted to do was
disappoint her man. She adored him. She lived for him.
She'd die for him, too.

"I'm sorry," Rachel groaned, tears welling in her eyes. "I didn't mean to."

Denny gnashed his teeth, "I don't care what you meant to do." He stared fire into her eyes, "Do what I *tell* you to do, you ungrateful *brat*."

Feelings overcame Rachel that she hadn't experienced since she was a child, staring into her father's eyes as he came home drunk—as he always did— and slammed her against a wall, telling her she was the biggest, ugliest, most ungrateful brat he had have had the displeasure of encountering. As Denny shook his head, uttered a stream of curses at his lover, Rachel felt something she hadn't felt in over ten years: fear.

"I'm sorry," she apologized to her man. "I won't disappoint you again."

"Pick up the gun," Denny barked. "Put a round into that copper's skull and you'll have my approval."

Rachel, hand searching the floormats, brushed her fingers against the grip of the gun. She secured it in both hands, cocking back the hammer and taking aim through the rear window. *Kill that cop*, she told herself. *Make your man proud.*

***

"Son of a gun," Mike uttered as he witnessed the woman taking aim through the windshield. He wasted no time and swerved the cruiser to the right, the woman volleying off a single shot that pinged off the roof of the car.

Mike came alongside the rear of the sedan. His tenure as a policeman had taught him a handful of things: how to spot a lie, how to shoot a gun, how to run, how to take cover, how to calm tense situations, and the best methods at staying alive. But the one thing in his arsenal of tactics that he was prepared to implement was one he had only done in training: the PIT maneuver. All it would require was lining up his front bumper to the rear tire of the sedan, tapping it, and sending it into a spin.

"Come on, buddy," Mike said to himself. "Let's get this thing done."

Mike recalled his training. He gripped the steering wheel, eased down on the accelerator, and lined up the front bumper with the rear of the sedan. The woman in the vehicle was attempting to take aim, Mike pressing down a little harder on the gas pedal and successfully tapping the rear end of the sedan. As he had hoped, the sedan lurched forward, spun in a circle, and the weapon fell clean out of the woman's grip as Mike slammed down hard on the breaks.

***

Rachel screamed as the sedan began to spin. She braced herself, Denny hollering out a stream of colorful curses as he struggled to gain control of the vehicle. A kaleidoscope blur of colors surrounded Rachel, her stomach twisting in a knot and the feeling that she might vomit causing her to close her eyes.

The sedan turned 360 degrees before coming to a stop. Denny, wasting no time, told Rachel to hand him the weapon as he kicked open the driver's side door. The sedan was parked perpendicular on the highway, as Rachel attempted to steady herself as she grabbed the gun and handed it over to her man.

Denny, glancing over his shoulder, spotted the cop throwing open the door to his cruiser. The cop, sporting a crème-colored uniform, stepped out of the cruiser, produced his sidearm, crouched down, and took cover behind his door.

"Let's go," Denny ordered Rachel. "I'm about to turn this prick into Swiss cheese."

Mike took aim at the male suspect. "Freeze!" he shouted. "Put your hands above your head and get down on your knees!"

The male suspect, gun in his hand, told Mike to stick it where the sun didn't shine as he lobbed off three rounds that punctured their way into the cruiser's door reinforced with steel plates. The sound of the shots punching the metal was like a sledgehammer being slammed down against an anvil, Mike ducking his head and cursing at himself for not taking the first shot. As soon as the shots died down, Mike spotted the male suspect dragging the female suspect by the arm toward the woods. He stood up, taking aim and trying to fire off a shot into the male suspect's legs—but the male suspect took cover behind a tree before Mike could squeeze the trigger.

Now we're in a standoff, Mike thought.

Outstanding.

***

Rachel trembled as she stayed in cover behind a towering oak tree. Denny, flexing his grip on his weapon, laughed as he hollered at the cop, "Come and get me."

"Denny baby," Rachel whispered. "What are we going to do?"

His free hand gripped around Rachel's arm, squeezing her tighter than he did before, Denny cursed again, "Shut your *damn mouth*, you ungrateful *sleaze*!"

Once again, Rachel felt like she was being chastised by her father. The feelings did not sit well with her. She loved Denny. She thought he was the greatest man she had ever met when so many men, like the one Denny had knocked down onto the dancefloor the night they met, had treated her like dirt. But the more they were boxed in, the closer the two of them brushed against death's door, the more she questioned whether Denny was the good a man she thought him to be. Feeling like she did the night she stood up to her father and told him to go to hell after he used his tagline of "ungrateful brat" for the very last time, Rachel looked at Denny with a fiery gaze, and demanded, "Be nice to me."

Denny squinted at her curiously, "What?"

"I said," Rachel mumbled, "be nice to me."

Mike shouted, "Come out! Let me see your hands!"

Denny fired a round blindly over his shoulder. "Damn cop," he smirked. "Between you and him, I don't know which one of you I'm going to shoot first."

The fingers on Rachel's hand curled into a fist. "I said," she repeated, "be nice to me."

Mike hollered, "Come out now!"

"Listen," Denny said to Rachel, "don't be an ungrateful slag, you hear me?"

Rachel had her fill of the situation. "Don't say it again," she ordered. "You know I hate being called that."

"I know," Denny laughed, "that's why I'm saying it."

"*Don't.*"

Denny fired another blind round at the cop. "Ungrateful," he mumbled.

"*Denny*," Rachel said. "One more time, and I'll—"

"And you'll *what?*" Denny said with a skeptical tone. "You'll do what, you *ungrateful* hag?"

Before her brain could register what her body was doing, Rachel shoved Denny out of cover. He fell to the ground, completely exposed with a wide-eyed gaze, looking like a deer in the headlights, as he raised his weapon toward the officer.

***

Mike couldn't believe what he was seeing – the woman shoved the male suspect out of cover. The male suspect now out in the open, raised his firearm to take aim as Mike planted his feet, stood tall, took aim, and squeezed the trigger.

Two gunshots registered—one from Mike, one from the male suspect. The suspect's bullet shattered the glass of Mike's window, the round a half-inch away from clipping his hip. The bullet from Mike's weapon drilled its way into the male suspect's sternum, throwing him onto his back with an air-depleted huff of his lungs.

The dust settled.

The smoke cleared.

Mike was the victor as the sound of the sirens coming to back him up rang out in the distance.

Rachel stared at Denny's body. Life had been snatched away from him in the blink of an eye. All she could think as she raised her hands above her head was, *That's the last time he'll call me ungrateful.*

The cop approached moments later with his weapon drawn. He threw Rachel onto the ground, cuffed her hands behind her back, and began reading her rights. He hauled her to his cruiser, tossing her in the back seat as a fleet of police cruisers showed up and parked at canted angles along the highway. As the police officers conversed and coordinated with the officer who put Denny down, Rachel stared at her (ex) lover's body lying sprawled on the ground. She *had* loved Denny. She *had* lived for Denny. At one point, she would have died for Denny—but that time had passed quicker than smoke dissipating in the wind.

Mike's father-in-law told him he was a hero. The man he put down, Denny Weems, was wanted for murder in two states. He did the right thing. He put a wild animal down, and the woman who was assisting him had warrants in various parts of the state. She would be locked up for the foreseeable future. Mike never wanted to be a cop—but he had learned he was quite good at it.

Night had arrived by the time Mike returned home; his utility belt draped over his shoulder as he padded his way toward the front door of his two-story home. His father-in-law gave Darlene the head's up of what happened, and Mike had suspected that his wife would throw open the front door and rush into his arms the moment he arrived back home, which is exactly what she did.

"Oh, my God," Darlene said as she coiled her arms around Mike's neck. "You're alright. Oh, honey! I was so scared."

Mike smiled and held his wife tight, "I'm fine, everything is going to be okay."

Darlene held his face in her hands, "I thought something terrible might have happened to you. Don't ever do that to me again, Mike. I don't know what we'd do without you."

"Same."

Darlene smiled, "Promise me," she demanded, "Tell me that you'll never put yourself in harm's way like that again."

Nodding, Mike answered, "Trust me. I've had enough excitement to last for a lifetime."

A tear streamed down Darlene's cheek as she pulled her husband in close, pressed her lips against his, and held onto the moment for as long as she possibly could.

A KISS OF NOSTALGIA

***

"With our tech, you can go back and recreate any moment of your life."

Carter, skeptical at the pitch, pinned his eyes to the salesman, "Like a VR experience?"

The salesman shook his head and steepled his fingers, "What we do here is far superior to that. VR is nothing more than a simulation. As good as the tech may be, you still have this sense lingering in the back of your mind that it's all a façade. At Echo, we tap into the part of your mind that houses your recollections, so to speak, and we enable you to reconstruct a specific memory and experience it as though it were happening in real time." A cool smirk spread across the salesman's lips, "You won't be able to tell the difference."

"Sounds too good to be true," Carter said.

"Most people are reticent the first time they come in here," the salesman offered. "It's only when they partake in the experience that they understand what we're selling." He held up a finger, "And we guarantee satisfaction or your money back. The experiences you have here are unapparelled."

Carter's lips curved into a grin, "Have you ever seen the movie *Total Recall*?"

The salesman furrowed his brow, "No, why?"

Carter waved his hand dismissively through the air, "Never mind."

"I can tell you're skeptical."

"I am," Carter admitted. "Honestly, I only came in here to see what the fuss was all about. Everyone's been taking part in this Echo trend lately." He sat back in his seat, "I'm curious. How many people have asked for a refund?"

Confidence oozed out of the salesman's eyes, "*No one.*"

Carter ogled the digital poster display on the wall inside the cramped office displaying a customer strolling through a dreamscape in wide-eyed amazement. "Partake in your past!" the placard read, "and remember with Echo!"

Too good to be true, his mind gibbered.

"Let's say that I do want to participate in this," Carter asked. "What kind of money am I going to be shelling out?"

"All of our sessions last one hour," the salesman said. "But for the user, depending on what memory they are reenacting, it can feel as though it's lasting for hours, days, weeks, maybe even months. The price for each session is a flat rate of $1,000."

The price tag elicited a whistle from Carter, "That's a lot."

"It is." The salesman shrugged, "But again, you'll understand why once you go through the experience."

The conversation Carter had with his older brother before leaving that morning came to mind: "Don't do it," Mikey said. "It's not a good idea."

"Why?" Carter asked.

"I think it's a bad idea."

"But I want to remember. I want to remember that time with, well, you know."

Mikey shook his head. "Don't, Carter. I'm begging you."

Carter asked, "Why?"

"It's better if you leave it in the past…"

The salesman laughed, "I can tell you're on the fence about it."

Carter inquired, "Can you blame me?"

"There has to be *something* from your past you want to go back over. Everyone has that one precious moment they want to recall."

There was only one memory Carter could think of that he never rectified in his mind. The more time that passed, the more Carter tried to pick through the commemoration like the proverbial needle in the haystack, the spottier it became. It was less clear, a shadow of what it once was. He knew he had made it a point to forget, but he couldn't remember why.

"Don't do it," Carter could hear Mikey saying. "Just leave it in the past."

"I can see it," the salesman pressed.

Carter wrinkled his brow, "See what?"

"See you trying to evoke the memory. It's like you have a word lingering on the tip of your tongue, one you're trying to mutter but can't seem to do so, and it's not for a lack of trying." The salesman gestured to the poster on the wall, "That's what we do here. We assist you in bridging the gap. We can help you reach that moment of catharsis you're so desperately yearning to have."

He's good, Carter thought. *He probably said this speech two-to-three times a day.*

The thought of retreading a path from the past, going back over something he so desperately wanted to sort out was tempting. But then he recalled Tom Portnoy from work going to Echo and coming back a shell of a man he once was. Portnoy used to be a happy guy, always smiling, continually viewing everything in life from a glass half full standpoint. But after Portnoy visited Echo for a session, he was never the same. No one knew what Portnoy had put himself through. Whatever it was, it cost him his job, his marriage, and eventually his sanity.

Just don't do it, Carter told himself. *Back away now. Mikey is right.*

"I think it's too much money," he offered, hoping to implement the most reasonable excuse. "I can't justify spending that much cash in one place, at the moment. I'm a blue-collar guy. My fiancé will have my head on a stake."

"If it's an issue of paying upfront," the salesman continued, "we offer weekly payment plans spread out according to your budget. All that would be required today is a down payment of $250."

"That's all?" Carter questioned, weighing his options once more in his mind.

The salesman nodded, "Yes, and once you give us the down payment and sign the agreement stipulating what your payment plan will be, we can get you in the pool."

With a wince radiating across his face, Carter said, "The pool?"

"Yes, that's what we call the area you're in for the session."

"Interesting."

The salesman asked, "Are you still not convinced?"

Carter replied, "A little worried, maybe."

"Why?"

Carter tried to remember why Mikey said he shouldn't do it. *What was it I'm forgetting?*

The salesman promised, "You don't need to worry. We are an upstanding institution with an immaculate track record."

Except for Tom Portnoy, Carter thought. *I wonder if this guy is hiding something from me.*

The salesman perched forward in his seat, "What do you have to lose, Mr. Dupree?"

"Nothing, I suppose."

"*Exactly.*"

"Well…what if I'm attempting to relive a more…*intimate* memory?"

"If you're worried about snooping on our end," the salesman promised, "I assure you that you do not have to fret. We don't monitor the memories as they're being played out. We simply keep an eye on your vital statistics. If we think you may be compromised in any fashion, we'll pull you out."

Carter asked, "Has anyone been, well, killed doing this? Injured?"

"No," the salesman assured, "We have had zero incidents since the technology was brought into existence."

Except for Tom Portnoy.

"I knew a man," Carter began. "He came to Echo one day. When he was finished, something happened to him."

A dour look spread across the salesman's face, "You're speaking of Mr. Portnoy."

Carter said, "You know him?"

The salesman nodded, "Yes, unfortunately. We were sad to hear that he was institutionalized after his time with us."

"I thought you said there were no negative repercussions with Echo."

The salesman wagged his finger, "I said there were no injuries or deaths with Echo. In the instance of Mr. Portnoy, he suffered a mental breakdown."

Carter laughed, "I'd say that counts as an injury, in a sense."

Sighing, "Can I be frank with you, Mr. Dupree?"

"As long as you don't call me 'Mr. Dupree.' Mr. Dupree was my father."

The salesman laughed, "Very well." He leaned back in his chair, "As I was saying, regarding the issue of Mr. Portnoy, he wasn't upfront with us about the memory he was attempting to relive. It's important here that people abide by the standards and procedures which have been deliberately put into place in order to protect our clients' well-being."

"What do you mean?"

"We don't allow clients to relive violent or potentially triggering memories. It wreaks havoc on the mind."

Carter asked, "How can you prevent someone from reliving whatever memory they want?"

The salesman replied, "We have safeguards in place. This is a finely-tuned science." He opened a drawer on the desk and produced a pamphlet with the Echo logo printed on the front, "You can read about the finer details of how the tech works in here."

Carter shook his head, "Again, I'm a blue-collar guy. All the tech terms will be lost on someone like me. Just explain it to me like you would a five-year-old."

Placing the pamphlet down, the salesman continued with his pitch. "The process is simple," he continued. "You tell us a key word that evokes the most potent response to the memory you are attempting to relive. Once you do, we use our tech to, in essence, pinpoint the memory. We home in on it, activate some…" he laughed, "*synapses* in your brain, so to speak, and boom, you're off and running. Think of it like we're looking at a map of your mind. When you utter the keyword, it causes all sorts of responses. That singular response is the X we use to mark on the map. Once we locate it, we open it up, in a manner of speaking."

"And all that takes is a single word?"

"Yes."

One word, Carter prattled. *That won't be hard to conjure up.*

"Then tell me," he said, "how Tom Portnoy ended up having a negative experience upon reliving his memory?"

"The word he used," the salesman answered. "We were under the impression that Mr. Portnoy was going to relive a cherished childhood memory after giving us the word. It turned out to be something that was, well, not-so-cherished. We are bound by NDAs here, but what I can say is the memory he ended up playing out was one that would cause anyone to endure a negative experience."

"You're saying that Tom Portnoy dug his own grave, in a sense?"

Shrugging, the salesman agreed, "You could say that, yes."

"So," Carter continued, "in a way, it's on me to make sure that I don't go down the wrong path?"

"Precisely. It's not that hard."

Maybe he's right, Carter thought. *Just think happy thoughts.*

"It's up to you," the salesman encouraged. "Again, I don't think you have anything to lose from this experience."

Carter took his time coming up with an answer. He considered all the options, recalled the moments of the memory he could still recount, and decided there was no harm in going back over the past as he pulled out his wallet and watched as the salesman took his card with a wide beaming smile stretching from one ear to the next.

***

"The pool" was a small, funnel shaped room with a reclining chair. The moment Carter stepped inside, he felt like he was entering a windowless therapist's office. A woman, dressed in something vaguely resembling a nurse's form, greeted him with a smile before gesturing to the chair.

"In here, please," she encouraged.

Carter approached the chair. Beside it was a cart that looked like the ones one might find in the ER wing of a hospital. A monitor and several computer-liked devices were on the cart along with a series of wires. A technician hovered over the monitor, clacking away at the keyboard and never acknowledging Carter once as he slipped down into the chair.

The nurse grabbed something that looked like a blood pressure monitor. "Did you sign your NDA?" she asked.

Carter smirked, "I did," as he thought about the six signatures he had to give to the salesman before entering the room.

"Very good," the nurse answered. "Now, I'm just going to take your vital statistics, and we can get started."

Carter glanced around the room as the nurse took his pulse and attached several stickers to his head. The stickers, small and black, glowed red as the nurse placed them on his forehead, his temples, and the back of his skull.

"It tingles," Carter said.

The nurse smiled warmly, "That's the equipment activating."

To Carter, it felt like a flurry of butterflies that were lying dormant in his mind start to come to life, caterpillars having gone through their metamorphosis stage and now bursting through the cocoon.

"Everything looks good," the tech said. "Digital map is rendered."

Carter clocked the monitor and saw a three-dimensional CT scan of his brain, "Weird."

"Now," the nurse reassured as she patted Carter's arm, "we need to clear your mind first. Saturating it with oxygen will help. Follow these next instructions carefully, okay?"

Carter nodded as the nurse led him through a one-minute breathing exercise: a deep breath in, a deep breath out, the process repeated several times before the nurse instructed him to blow all the air out of his lungs and hold it for thirty seconds. When the time was up, Carter drew in a breath, held it for fifteen seconds, and blew it all out. When he was finished, he felt a warm sensation spread through his body akin to that of slipping into a hot tub.

The nurse queried, "How do you feel?"

Endorphins firing on all cylinders, Carter replied, "Not bad."

"Good." The nurse nodded to the tech, "Are you ready?"

The tech replied, "I just need his word."

"Now, Mr. Dupree," the nurse instructed, "I need you to take a minute. Close your eyes, recall the memory we are going to exhume, and think of an object, any object that stands out in this memory. Focus on it for a solid moment. Once you can see it clearly in your mind, call it out, and then we will begin the process."

Carter said, "How will I know when I've gone under?"

The nurse replied, "You'll know."

"When will I come back out?"

"Just repeat the word that you're about to tell us when you're in the memory. Once you say it, you'll be out in the blink of an eye. Okay?"

Nodding, Carter said, "Okay."

"Good," the nurse said. "Whenever you want to, you can begin."

Closing his eyes, Carter began to scour through his mind. It was fuzzy at first, like driving down a desolate highway blanketed with a thick layer of fog. After a moment, he could see the object in his mind – a rose.

The nurse said, "Do you see it, Mr. Dupree?"

Nodding, Carter declared, "I do."

"Then whenever you're ready…"

Carter could practically feel the golf ball in his hand. He could sense its texture, feeling himself back in the moment when he picked it up and rolled it in his hand, and drawing a deep breath, he then spoke the word, "*Rose.*"

Carter peeled open his eyes. The sun was shining brightly overhead. The wind was blowing. He looked down and saw himself standing next to his beige VW Jetta. It took him a moment to calibrate, to realize he was submerged in his memory. He glanced down at his clothes, the style he was sporting ten years out of season. His hair was longer. He was twenty pounds lighter. The beard on his face was now gone.

"Holy shit," Carter whispered. "It worked..."

He turned in a circle and found himself standing outside a five-story apartment complex in San Francisco, the view of the Golden Gate Bridge just off in the distance.

I haven't lived here in years, Carter thought as a familiar sense of his surroundings began to come back to him.

After a moment, it occurred to Carter he wasn't in his neighborhood. The apartment he used to live in was three miles away. Taking in the building on his right, he recalled whose apartment complex it was, and his heart began to race as the doors to the lobby opened and a young woman stepped out from inside.

It's her, Carter's mind chattered. *Oh, my God, it's her.*

The young woman smiled. She was dressed in blue jeans, a black top, and a colorful scarf wrapped around her neck. Carter recalled the scarf well, as it occurred to him, according to his memory, he would be removing that scarf from her neck later on that night.

"Hi!" the young woman giggled.

Carter was stunned. His heart was racing. His mouth was open. The young woman embraced him, and Carter held her tight and felt as though he were free-falling.

"It's nice to see you again," the young woman bubbled.

Carter took in her features, the beauty mark on her upper lip, her hazel eyes staring at him with wide-eyed enthusiasm. "*Alex*," he said.

The young woman, Alex, giggled again. "That's my name, yeah."

"It's so good to see you."

Alex squeezed his hand, "I've never had a second date a day after the first."

That's right! Carter thought. *We met for coffee the day before!*

"Same," he said.

Alex wrinkled her brow, "Are you alright?"

Carter couldn't come to terms with the fact that it was nothing more than a memory. He could feel Alex's body brushing up against him. He was picking up on the scent of her perfume. It was intoxicating, a scent he had long-since forgotten but was now experiencing in crystal-clear detail.

We fall in love, he thought. *We make love until the sun rises every day. We're inseparable. Attached at the hip...but what happened? What went wrong? Why did we not stay together?*

Carter blinked himself out of his trance, "Sorry," he paused, "You just look so...*beautiful.*"

Alex blushed, "And you look very handsome...very dapper."

It dawned on Carter that he was with Samantha back in the "real world." His fiancé – the woman he vowed to spend the rest of his life with. *Is this cheating?* he thought. *Should I even be here? No, I shouldn't be...but it's just a memory. It's not even real!*

For a moment, Carter thought about sending out a signal to the tech back at Echo. Maybe they could pull him out. It wasn't too late to—

"*Hey*," Alex cooed as she took Carter's hand into her own, "you look dazed."

The sensation of the young woman's hand sent shockwaves through Carter's body. In all of an instant, he let go of his hang ups and pulled Alex in close.

"Can I kiss you?" he asked.

Alex responded by closing her eyes and bringing her face close to his. Carter pressed his lips against hers and felt a wave of euphoria overcome him. *I remember you*, he told himself. *I remember how you feel. I remember every inch of who you are.*

The kiss seemed to last for an eternity. Carter thought about nothing else as he forgot his life back in the real world and proceeded to open the passenger's side door to his car. He opted to spend just a couple of hours with Alex, to relive a few high notes from his time with her before he headed back home.

I'll leave tonight, he thought. *Before we enter that house, I'll say the word 'rose' again. That's the smart thing to do.*

***

Carter spent the day traversing the city with Alex. There was no end in sight to his reminiscence. Though there was a familiar sense of everything they did, down to the sights and smells, it was as if Carter was experiencing it all for the first time. It was like a lingering essence of *déjà vu* was in the air as they went to the fish markets, to a local bookstore, to a bar where they shared cocktails until the sun began its descent into the west. By the time the drinks were finished, six hours had passed—and Carter didn't want it to end.

Alex led Carter by the hand to the front door of her apartment. Her eyes flickered as she brought him to the entryway, her arms wrapping around his waist as the two of them kissed passionately with no end in sight.

"You can stay the night," Alex whispered into his ear.

Her breath was hot on his neck, the hairs standing on end as Carter recalled his promise to himself to utter the word "rose." *I need to leave*, he told himself. *I can't go through with this.* But no matter how much Carter protested, no matter how hard he tried, he couldn't pull himself away from the memory.

"Carter," Alex said, "do you want to come in?"

Carter cupped her face in his hands. He smiled. He nodded and told himself he could stay a little while longer. *Why can't I?* he thought. *I can go back home whenever I want. I can live out this memory as long as I wish! Nothing went wrong with Alex. I probably just made a mistake I can*

fix! I can stay here...forever.

Nodding, Carter took Alex by the hand and walked

into her apartment. He closed the door behind them as Alex

palmed the light switch off, and Carter began to slowly peel

the scarf off from around her neck. They spent the night

together, Carter promising to himself once again he would

say the word "rose" the moment that he awoke. But he

didn't—he would end up staying a total of three more

months, convinced it would continue to play out as long as

Carter wished.

But it didn't.

***

Alex looked at Carter curiously as they strolled

down the sidewalk outside her apartment. When they

awoke that day, three months into their relationship, a

sickly feeling overcame Carter, and he wasn't sure why. He

felt off, out-of-place, wondering what was wrong with him and having completely forgotten the fact that he was living out a memory. At this point, it was his reality. He was certain the memories of going into the salesman's office at Echo, at being tethered to the machine was nothing more than a figment of his imagination.

"Something's wrong," Alex said with a frown. "Something's wrong with all of this."

Carter shook his head, "Nothing's wrong, baby." He kissed her on the cheek, "We're exactly where we're supposed to be."

Alex pulled her hand away from Carter's, "No," she paused. "I…I have this…this odd feeling, this feeling like we're not supposed to be here."

"Why do you say that?"

A grimace was now on Alex's face, "This is wrong. This isn't how it happened."

Something caught Carter's eye in the horizon – the clouds. They appeared to be melting. *What the hell?* he thought. *My mind must be playing tricks on me.*

"I have to go, Carter," Alex said as she gestured to the sidewalk at the end of the block just ten paces away.

"Why?" Carter asked. "We're going the other direction, remember?"

Alex shook her head, "No, we don't go that way." She jutted her chin to the sidewalk, "We go *this* way. That's how it ends. Don't you remember?"

It occurred to Carter that Alex no longer sounded like Alex. Her voice was familiar, but it was one that didn't belong to her.

I know that voice, he said. *I've heard it before. But who does it belong to?*

"You forgot, Carter," Alex said. "You forgot how this ends."

Heart beating wildly in his chest, Carter began to recall he was in a memory, that everything he was experiencing was nothing more than a dream. *She's right,* he told himself. *Oh, my God. She's right. I know how this play outs. I made it a point to forget.* Heart in his throat, Carter realized Mikey was right when he told him not to go.

"I have to go," Alex said. "You know how this has to end."

That's the trauma therapist's voice, Carter recalled. *She was the one who helped me after...after...*

Carter shook his head as Alex approached the sidewalk. He reached out toward her, begging her to come back. He wanted to run after her, to pull her back but his feet just wouldn't budge. He felt glued to the concrete, watching as Alex stepped into the crosswalk. Tears streamed down his face as he screamed out Alex's name, and a moment later, the bus that ended up taking her life came careening down the street. Right before the vehicle made contact, Carter hollered at the top of his lungs, "Rose!"

***

Carter's eyelids fluttered. He awoke to find himself in the pool at the Echo offices. The first thing he saw was the digital clock on the wall. Just like the salesman had stated, only an hour had passed since he first went under. In his mind, he had been gone for months. In reality, that was not the case.

The nurse who had tethered Carter to the machine pulled the stickers off of his head. "How do you feel?" she asked.

Carter said nothing. All he could see was the bus that had collided into Alex, taking her away from him before their relationship could fully blossom. He continued to say nothing as he was led out of the pool, the salesman concerned, encouraged Carter to go to the hospital. Carter continued to replay the memory over and over as he was checked out by the doctors.

It went on even after he returned home to his fiancé. It didn't wane in the days that followed as Carter slipped into a catatonic state. The days turned into weeks. The weeks turned into months. By the time a year had passed, Carter, still reliving the trauma, was forced to go into therapy at the same institution Tom Portnoy now called home. After a year and a half, with no progress being made, Carter was locked into a room with Tom Portnoy where he lived out his days dwelling in a memory that should have remained buried.

AN IMPRACTICAL KISS

***

Russ Elliot was certain Charlie didn't know he existed.

Well, not in a literal sense. He sat beside her in enough

classes that she had to know by this point he was a living,

breathing human being. Chances were good she knew his

name. She probably recognized his face. But Charlie was

completely unaware of the fact that Russ was head-over-

heels for her, admiring her from a distance but not in a

creepy sense. He didn't have pictures on his phone. He

didn't steal articles of her clothing like some kind of BTK

enthusiast. Sure, he looked at her social media feed every

once in a while, but the affection Russ felt for Charlie was

limited to holding a special place for her in his heart. He

adored her—but he knew there was nothing he could do

about it.

Mrs. Kline, addressing the entire class, was in the throes of explaining something about the Spanish Civil War. For Russ, seated next to Jacob in the back of the room, every word Kline spoke might as well have been Spanish. He was too fixated on trying not steal a furtive glance at Charlie. She was in the second row from the front, as she always was, her best friend Kylie on her left and second-best friend Jordanna on her right. All Russ could make out was the back of Charlie's head, her flowing brunette hair catching the light filtering in through the windows on the left.

She's an angel, Russ told himself. *As cheesy as it sounds, it's true.*

Charlie used her pen to flick back her hair. She did that about three times during each period. Russ caught a glimpse of her neckline, his heart fluttering like the wings of a hummingbird.

I wish I could say how I feel, he thought. *I wish I could—*

What sounded like the crack of a whip resonated in Russ's right eardrum. He shuddered, the entire class turning around to lay eyes on the commotion. Straightening his posture, Russ angled his body toward Jacob. Hand to his stomach, Jacob was chuckling, and in his other hand was the twisted-up plastic straw that he had tied into a knot and then proceeded to relieve the air pressure it built up by flicking the knot and causing the straw to snap. It was the second time that week Jacob had pulled the stunt and managed to stir a rise out of Russ.

"*Idiot,*" Russ whispered to Jacob.

Mrs. Kline cleared her throat. "Jacob," she grumbled. "Russell. Is there a problem?"

Jacob shrugged. He held up the straw and gestured to it like an antique's appraiser. "My straw broke, Mrs. Kline. Stupid thing is on the fritz."

A few kids laughed. Most of them rolled their eyes or mumbled for Jacob to shut up. That's how it usually went. Jacob—who Russ was certain had a career in stand-up comedy—was always trying out new jokes or pranks that would pave the way to some kind of career later down the line. The way he dressed (white shorts with a Budweiser logo, knee-high-socks, and an oversized shirt with Pauly Shore's face and the words "Wheeze the Juice" printed on the front), the curled, shoulder length-hair, and the perpetual and devious grin on his face made him—in the Vice Principal's own words—a character.

Mrs. Kline placed her hands on her hips. "Enough, Jacob," she said. "You too, Russ. I'm not in the mood."

Russ bid his apologies. Jacob held up his hands in surrender. At one point, Russ caught Charlie looking back at him quizzically. It was the first time she had done so, perhaps ever. He quickly averted his gaze. The rhythm of his heart was beating so fast that it made the 40 minutes remaining in the class feel more like four.

***

Russ, with Jacob in tow, filed out of the classroom with the sea of other students out in the hallway. The final bell had rung. School, as Alice Cooper was stated, was (almost) out for the summer. Just four more days and they would graduate and go on to the next phase of their lives. Most of the students at LC would traverse the globe for the summer. Some would go off to college. A majority of them would stay behind and follow in their affluent parents' footsteps of becoming real estate agents or real estate attorneys buying and selling the same, multi-million-dollar properties over and over again like some rich, insipid version of the film *Groundhog Day.* But Russ wasn't like those kids. Neither was Jacob. The only reason they went to LC was because it touted the proud seal of a "Blue Ribbon" school. It was, allegedly, a prestigious institution that paved the way toward to ushering in the younger generation into positions of prominence. It was how Dr. Lance Kline (Mrs. Kline's husband), the principal, had phrased it to the point of exhaustion. But what did he know? Dickhead had his PHD in Phys Ed., but the way he composed himself, one would have taken the Mitt Romney lookalike for a brain surgeon. Point being, Russ and Jacob's parents wanted their sons to retain a good education that would allow them to break their middle-class molds, however, being the average price of a property in LC clocked in at a base rate of $1.5 million, they rented their properties, hence the wealthier kids lumping Russ and Jacob into the "subpar" category of a brood unenthusiastically coined "the renters."

Jacob and Russ filed out of the main building toward the parking lot. Russ, taking a moment to scan for signs of Charlie, came up short.

"Why'd you do that?" Russ said.

Jacob furrowed his brow, "Do what, bruh?"

"Flick that stupid straw in my ear."

Jacob shrugged, "Cause it was funny."

The stealthy glance Charlie took of Russ back in class plagued his mind as if he had committed a sin. "I looked like an asshole," he said. "Everyone was staring at me."

"You didn't look like an asshole," Jacob assured him as he fished his car keys out of his pocket.

Russ said, "I didn't?"

Jacob shook his head. "No, you looked like a pussy boy. But pussy boys have their place in this world. I'm proud to know a pussy boy."

Russ fired off a smirk, "Thanks, man."

"Anytime." Jacob patted his buddy on the back, "That's what I'm here for."

The two arrived at a matte-painted Pinto, second-hand gifted to Jacob by his older brother after he went off to Washington to work at a brewery after graduating five years earlier. Jacob referred to the Pinto as "the canvas," a graffiti-tagged monstrosity that looked as though it had been vandalized. But it wasn't. It looked like some kind of Eddie Van Halen, Franken Strat-inspired cacophony of colors because Jacob allowed the other students to spray-paint whatever they wanted onto the car or slap a bumper sticker on simply the sake of doing so. After three years of "artwork" being appended to the vehicle, Jacob had been pulled over three times by the cops simply out of curiosity.

Jacob nodded over his shoulder, "You want to get some za, brah?"

Russ sighed, "Dude…"

"What?"

"Stop calling it that."

A mischievous twinkle glimmered in Jacob's eyes, "You don't like za, brah?"

"Just call it 'pizza'," Russ said. "You only say 'za' because it's annoying as shit."

Jacob crossed his eyes and stuck out his tongue. He spoke in a tone adjacent to an animated Disney gremlin, "Get some *za, brah*! Big ole sloppy slice to shove in your face hole."

Russ peeled open the passenger's side door, "Let's get Panda Express. I haven't had that in a minute. That cashew shrimp thing coated with honey is supposed to be good."

"I'm down for that," Jacob said as he slid behind the wheel. "We need to talk anyway."

"About what?"

A laugh puttered out of Jacob's lips, "About that Bundy-esque way you were ogling Charlie today."

Russ' stomach twisted into a knot. "I wasn't staring at her," he said defensively.

"You're *always* staring at her. You gotta quit it with that 'watching from a distance' shit. Just ask her out. We're out of here in four days anyway. If she says no, so what?"

"I'm not like you, man," Russ said defeatedly. "I don't have the balls to do something like that. Besides, she's going to Cal Tech. Some shit bird with a startup is probably going to swoon her the second she steps foot on campus."

"*Swoon?*" Jacob said. "God damn, bruh. You *do* read too much."

The same had been said about Russ his entire life. Ever since the fourth grade, his nose was jammed spine-deep into a book. Sports didn't intrigue him. Even though he had the scrawny build that most of the math aficionados had, his hopes to strive past solving even the most basic of equations was a pipedream at best. English and history were his strong suits. He knew he wanted to be a writer one day. It would just take him until college to figure out that jotting down short stories in a journal at night were the early symptoms flagging down his affliction.

Jacob slid behind the wheel. "Besides," he said, "in regard to Charlie, you don't have balls to begin with, pussy boy. I'm not a doctor but chances are high that you'll sprout some nuggets if you *try.*" He slipped the key into the ignition and then held up a finger, "Actually, I *am* a doctor."

Knowing what was coming next, and very much wanting to hear the punchline, Russ, an amused look on his face, said, "Doctor of what?"

Cranking the engine to life, the radio inside belting out "When I Meet My Maker," Jacob smashed his eyebrows together, and said, "Doctor of crushing pu—"

"*Hey!*" a voice called out.

Russ closed his eyes as the piano intro to the song played out. Dani Mayer's voice was all-too familiar (and excruciating at this point). Turning his head, he pinned his eyes to the four-foot-tall bridge troll with a penchant for being the premier affluent girl on campus striving to right the wrongs of the world. Oppression and misdeeds of the human domain, in her words, "running rampant," Dani's self-appointed role was one of spearheading change, her "achievements" limited to elaborate social media posts designating her "cause of the week," and the number of likes she procured a point of pride. It didn't matter what you said or whether you were on her side or not, Dani managed to always point out what you were doing wrong, how you could do better, and even if you managed to fulfill her expectations, the goal posts continued to change. Knowing Dani since the third grade, it took Russ until Sophomore year to understand she was simply scrambling to find relevance in an affluent community where she blended in with the other rich girls like mayo in a cup of expired yogurt.

"Russel," Dani said, "Jacob. I need a moment."

Jacob groaned, "I can peel out now."

Russ shook his head, "Na, man. She'll flag you down to the office for speeding."

"She's done that twice." Jacob patted the roof, "She's already tried to get my rig towed for being an 'environmental hazard.'"

It was too late—Dani's head was partway into the car. An iPad was clutched her hand. Her tee-shirt proudly displaying the words "Ally for People of Color."

"Can you turn that down?" Dani asked, wincing at the radio like she had just sucked on a lemon.

Jacob shook his head, "Volume button is busted. My fat ass backed in the wrong way a week ago and smashed in the knob."

Dani rolled her eyes. She thrusted the iPad toward Russ, "I need you to sign this."

"Let me guess," Jacob said, "some mongoloid whale beached itself last week and we need to go throw water on it."

Russ closed his eyes. Jacob only implanted terms like "mongoloid" simply to get a rise out of people like Dani. He didn't mean it. He just didn't like her. Dani provided plenty of reasons for this to be the case.

The whites of Dani's eyes were showing, "*What* did you say? Did you just use a derogatory term for people with *mental disabilities*?"

Jacob's eyes scanned the interior of the car like he was looking for a Post-It note with the answer scribbled on it. "Uh, *yeah*," he said. "I was going to use the Big R word instead, but last time I did, you reported me to the office, and I had to go to a sensitivity class for a week."

The vein in Dani's forehead protruded, "And I'm going to report you again," she said. "In the meantime," she waved the iPad around, "I need you to sign this petition. The school has overlooked a gross incompetence that needs to be rectified."

Russ, resting his head back on his seat, "What is it this time?"

"I've rallied a local artist, who just made his mark on TikTok" Dani said, "to paint a mural of an El Salvadorian girl. Her story is inspirational. I feel it's necessary to paint a mural honoring her on the outside of the gym. The school, in all their incompetence, has stated that the price tag of $10,000 is too high a price to pay to honor her."

Jacob closed his eyes. "Dani," he said, "this is stupid."

"*Stupid*," Dani spat, "is not rallying our efforts and marching on school grounds to right this wrong, which we will be doing this afternoon. I expect you to be there."

"Or you'll report me," Jacob said. "Correct?"

Dani nodded, a smug beam stretching from one ear to the next. "That's right," she said.

Jacob clapped his hands together. "Let me get this straight: you'll be reporting me for saying mongoloid, you'll report me for not signing your petition or marching with you, because I'm not doing either. Do I have this all right?"

Holding her head high, Dani intoned, "You got it."

Jacob put the car into reverse. "Hey," he said with glee, "why stop there?"

Russ knew what was coming next. He buckled up as Jacob smashed his foot into the gas pedal and threw the car into reverse. Dani backed out of the way, the tires of the Pinto whisking up smoke as Jacob peeled out of the lot in a 180-manuver, Dani (for whatever reason) screaming "Assault!" at the top of her lungs as Jacob cranked up the volume of the music and Russ held on for the ride.

***

The usual kids from school were at the Panda Express—much to Russ' dismay. In terms of school politics, cliques, friend groups, and all the little petty social classes that everyone fell into, Russ had managed to break down the different groups by the time he reached his Junior year. He ended up drafting what amounted to a dissertation on the sociology behind the groups. Had he known at the time that it was something his history teacher Mr. Gruber would have raised a brow at upon reading, he wouldn't have kept it buried under the stacks of journals, notebooks, and word documents he drafted that Russ kept under lock and key.

"There are several groups one can find traversing the LC campus," Russ had jotted down in his journal. "As much as the times have changed, the politics of the world infiltrating the campus and redefining the tropes and cliches, many of the factions remain the same as they have in the past twenty years."

"You have the jocks. They haven't changed much. I prefer to call them 'the meatheads.' This fraternity of 'brothers' spanning all the different sports still operates with a kind of low-brow mentality and alpha male swagger."

"There are also the brainiacs. The smart ones. The bookworms. They're all in the same group. These people are the best and brightest, looked down upon, mostly ignored, by all of the other factions. The brainiacs stick to their own kind. They discuss theories and equations and everything else in-between, paving the way for illustrious careers they will have later down the line. If one took the time to get to know them, which I have, you find they are possibly the friendliest people you ever met—save for

David Turner. As smart as he is, all he does is talk about *Star Wars*. It's kind of off-putting."

"You have the wealthy girls—the cheerleaders, 'influencers,' 'activists,' and vapid, breeze-brained Stepford-league women. I lump them all into the same category. They're very interchangeable. You can spot them coming from a million miles away. These girls tend to link-up and pair off with the meatheads."

"There are also the freaks—the emo kids, the punk rock kids, the ones who are into skateboarding. Their uniform is always the same: variants of black, long greasy hair, painted nails, a record for multiple suspensions and even expulsions. They're a bit standoffish at first, but some of them, once you break through the mold, can tend to welcome you in, if even for a minute."

"There are the surfer boys. I call them the 'Chili Peppers.' These are your typical, Orange County league dipshits on their way to joining a fraternity. They're a subdivision of the meatheads minus the penchant for playing sports. If not for that, they're almost interchangeable, and some tend to pair off with the affluent girls."

The last group Russ had identified were known as "The Outliers." The odd ones. Ones who didn't fit into any particular group. There were only a select few of these kinds of people, and Russ found that he and Jacob were a part of this group. They had the ability to sort of "float" from one group to the next like Jane Goodall shadowing chimps for the sake of science. Had Russ been aware at the time that the Outliers where the gifted ones, he would have known falling into this group would ended up paving the way towards his career as a writer later in life.

Russ and Jacob, entering the Panda Express, saw "representatives" from many of the different groups gathering for a meal. Russ, smirking as he scanned the crowd, couldn't help but feel it was fate that brought them all here just four days before they all graduated.

Jacob nudged Russ in the ribs, "What are you doing?"

Russ shrugged. "Just playing witness," he said. "It's funny, I'm not going to miss most of these people. Some of them, sure, but I'll forget most of their names within a year."

"You know," Jacob said, "you're a weird guy, man."

Russ nodded, "I know. I prefer it that way."

Gesturing toward the food in the display cases, Jacob said, "Come on. Let's get something to eat."

***

The Pinto was parked in the country club overlooking the entirety of the city. Orange hues painted the sky. Dusk was turning into night. Russ, downing the last of his Coke in the Panda Express cup, sighed and leaned back against the windshield.

Jacob, dancing in place as the car radio softly hummed out "True Love" by Glenn Frey, squinted at the horizon. "Think Dani will report me?" he asked.

Russ shrugged, "Probably. But they won't do anything. We graduate in four days. They don't want to cause a stink, so they'll probably just reprimand you and call it even."

Pouting his lip in approval, "I can live with that."

Russ sighed, "Man, Dani is just like all the other turds in this stupid ass school. I'm stoked we're getting out of here."

Jacob laughed, "We're going to community college, dingus. It's like ten minutes from here."

"Still," Russ said, "it'll be a nice change of pace. We're ten years behind the times, man." He nodded to the car radio churning out Glenn Frey. "We were born in the wrong decade, dude. No one ever got us. At least we survived though if you know what I mean."

"Spoken like a true idiot," Jacob said. "But you're right. Between Dani and all the other dipshits, even the clowns we'll probably run into at PCC will be a breath of fresh air, at least for a quick minute."

Russ propped himself up on his elbow, "You still going to do graphic design? You were on the fence last week."

"Only because of my bio dad," Jacob groaned. "He wants me to split and go back to Michigan for a minute." He swiped his hand through the air, "Screw that. I'll stick out with my mom and my sister. What about you? You haven't picked your classes out yet."

"Yeah," Russ said. "I just don't know what I want to do. I'll figure it out. I'm not some lost soul in need of meaning. I just can't focus."

Jacob crooked a finger, "Because you're focused on Charlie."

"Let it *go*, man."

"No, *you* can't let it go, Russ. You've been all about that girl since elementary school."

It was true. Russ remembered the day he first met Charlie. His parents had just moved to town in a bid to get him and his sister Angela into a better school. Angela had long-since graduated High School and moved to Italy with her fiancé. She was nearly seven years older than Russ, so when they moved to the city, it was more difficult for her to adapt than it had been for Russ. She had started in the 8th grade, the "formative years." But she learned to adapt. It was Russ who actually had a harder time in the long run.

When Russ entered the playground, almost as if it had been staged, Charlie had zipped out of the slide on the playground near his feet. The two collided into one another, Russ was taken off of his feet and Charlie offered up her apologies in reply. He had never cared much for girls before, but the second Charlie stood up, his stomach felt like it was filled with butterflies.

"I'm sorry!" Charlie apologized. "Are you okay?"

All Russ did in reply was nod and grin sheepishly. Charlie waved at him, said she was sorry, and then proceeded to rejoin her friends at the top of the slide. For two days, he barely spoke, infatuated with Charlie but for reasons he could not understand. It made it nearly impossible for him to make friends, but the moment that he partnered up his second week in school with Jacob…well,

it was all downhill after that. The two boys were, as Russ'
late grandmother might say, "Peas in a pod."

Russ always liked Charlie. He kept his distance. He
made sure never to be weird, creep her out, or do anything
other than catch a quick glimpse of her now and again. The
more time went on, the more beautiful Charlie became, not
just in appearances but in spirit.

How could anyone not *like her?* he thought many a
time. *She's smart. She's not vapid like the other girls. She's
kind. Welcoming. I just never grew the stones to say
anything about it.*

"It's because of her," Jacob said, bringing Russ out
of his trance, "that you've never been on a date, never been
to a dance—"

"—Neither have you," Russ cut in.

"*Point being,*" Jacob continued, "I think you need to
purge yourself or whatever. Charlie's a distraction, dude.

You need to just step up, say how you feel, and roll with the punches."

Russ slid off the hood of the Pinto. He slipped his hands into his pockets. He puttered his lips and stared at the sprawling sea of homes nestled into the mountainside. "You know what gets me?" he said. "The fact that she *will* say no. She's on a different journey than me. She'll go to Cal Tech, get a degree for being a genius, and then cure cancer or something. But that doesn't bother me. I'll be bummed she's gone, sure. It'll suck not being able to see her walk in and out of classes every day…but I just wish I said something so I would know for sure that she said 'no' to me asking her out or whatever. At least I'll have closure."

Jacob threw up his hands, "Are you hearing yourself?"

Russ angled his body toward Jacob, "What about it?"

"You just gave yourself your answer!" Jacob barked. "You know what you have to do. I mean, for crying out loud, man. If this were a movie, you're the hero in the third act who finally figured out what he needs to do to…be *free*, or whatever."

The light clicked on inside of Russ' brain, illuminating everything he was thinking and feeling in crystal, 4k resolution.

"Holy shit," he proclaimed. "I'm an idiot. I can't believe I had the answer in my head the whole time. I just…needed to say it out loud or whatever."

Jacob rapped his knuckles on the roof of the Pinto. "Then let's go!" he said. "She's probably still at school for that valedictorian crap they're doing at graduation. We go there, you talk to her, she shoots you down, and then we go back to my place to watch the Rick James sketch again for the millionth time."

The proposition was so simple, so elegant. *Why not? Russ told himself. She's going to say no. She'll probably be nice about it, too. I'll have my answer.*

A grin worked itself into Russ' expression, "Let's do it.,"

Cackling, Jacob opened the driver's side door.

That's when the security guard for the country club approached.

"You two," the guard said. "What are you doing here? You're trespassing. I'm calling the police."

"Uh…" Jacob began. "We don't speak English."

The guard sighed, "You don't speak English?"

Jacob shook his head, "No. English…no good…we…we very lost…help us."

"Knock it off."

A laugh trickled out of Jacob's mouth, "Take it easy."

Pointing his flashlight, the guard then said, "How about I take you down to the central county jail? Huh?"

Russ recognized the guard's voice. Taking a step closer, he squinted and made out a face he had seen before. "Troy Harlow?" he said. "Is that you, man?"

Jacob's eyes were wide. "No *way!*" he said. "Harlow, didn't you get expelled for mooning the soccer team junior year?"

The guard, Troy, puffed his chest. "That was a long time ago, jackass."

"People don't forget."

"Get out of here."

"Why are you working *here*?" Jacob said. "is Mickey D's not hiring or something?"

Troy's face turned a ruby shade of red. "I'm warning you two idiots," he grumbled. "Get lost. Now!"

Jacob, still laughing, "Didn't you crap your pants in the locker room that one time—?"

"*Go!*" Troy shouted.

Chuckling and running toward the Pinto, Jacob and Russ left the parking lot as Troy uttered a steam of curses.

***

Jacob pulled the Pinto into the school parking lot. Russ could see the students on the platform erected in front of the bleachers on the football field. His nerves were on edge. He always imagined what the day would look like when he confessed how he felt to Charlie, but it never looked like this.

"So," Jacob said as he put the shifter into park, "what do you want to do?"

Russ shrugged, "I guess I just…go onto the field and talk to her."

"You're not going to crap your pants, are you?"

Russ shot Jacob a quizzical look, "*What?*"

"You know," Jacob said, "because of your nerves, or whatever."

"I'm not going to crap my pants, dickhead."

"You might pass out."

"Shut up."

"You might go into a seizure, even. I heard about this kid back in Michigan. He asked this girl out to prom, and when the girl said no," Jacob snapped his fingers, "the kid just spazzed out and fell right to the ground."

Russ rolled his eyes, "I'm not going to flip out, man. I got this."

"You sure?"

Russ nodded, "Yeah, man. Just wait here for me. I'm sure I'll be back in a flash."

Jacob reached over and rested his hand on Russ' shoulder. "Hey," he said.

Russ looked at Jacob.

"I'm proud of you," Jacob said. "Jokes aside, I know this probably isn't easy."

Smirking, Russ said, "Thanks, dude. That means a lot."

Jacob, closing his eyes slowly, parted his lips, leaned across the sear, and said, "Quick kiss?"

Russ pushed Jacob out of the way. Jacob laughed as Russ got out of the car and smoothed the wrinkles in his white tee-shirt. Russ' style that hadn't changed in four years – white shirt and jeans. He didn't care for fashion. Didn't care for much else save for spending time with his family, Jacob, reading, and thinking about Charlie.

Maybe that will change today, he told himself. *Maybe this is one of those, what do you call it, milestone moments. Whatever happens here, I'll go onto the next phase of my life.*

Russ knew it was silly. Charlie wasn't going to let him down easily, and again, he didn't mind. He wasn't some lovesick soul who invested all of his attention and energy into someone he had a crush on. Russ wasn't like most kids—he was smart, self-aware, capable enough to handle his emotions at a level of someone ten years his senior. He was just…hung up on Charlie. That was all. But once he approached her. Once he talked to her. Once he said what he needed to say, got his "no, thank you," in reply, all would be right in the world.

The football field was a mere 100 yards away. Holding his chin high, Russ proceeded to the metal gate cordoning off the field from the parking lot, spotted Charlie decorating the stage that had been erected with the colors of the school, and proceeded to do what he needed to do.

The closer that Russ came to Charlie, the more he started to sweat. He thought about what to say, how to say it, thought about backing away and calling it quits but his feet simply wouldn't let him.

Charlie was twenty feet away now.

Do it, Russ said.

Fifteen feet away.

You got this.

Five feet away.

Just get it all over with.

Russ, two feet away from Charlie, felt frozen in place. She turned around, her eyes wide and a pleasant smile on her face and a bit startled upon seeing Russ standing before her.

"Oh!" she said. "Hey, Russ."

A silly smirk was on Russ' face, "You…know my name?"

Charlie laughed,. "Of course, I do." She glanced around. "What, uh…what's up? Are you okay?"

Russ stuck his hands in his pockets to stave off the shakes. "Yeah, sorry," he said as he hung his head. "This is weird, I know. I, uh, hope I'm not interrupting anything."

Charlie shook her head, "We're just doing some decorating." She glanced over her shoulder, "I don't mean to be rude, but I don't think you're supposed to be on the field."

Holding up his hands, Russ took a step back, "You're right. This is weird. I don't even know you and I'm just…walking right up to you and starting a conversation."

Charlie furrowed her brow. "You're such an odd guy, Russ. You always have been."

Turning away and admitting defeat, Russ said, "I know. I'm working on my social skills."

"Tell me."

"Tell you what?" Russ said curiously.

Charlie crossed her arms, "You know," tucking a loose strand of her hair behind her ear, "I'm not stupid."

Russ shook his head, "You're the opposite, actually. You're in Honor English, History, and...well, everything."

"Point being," Charlie said, "I know that you've, I guess you could say, noticed me before."

The rhythm of Russ' heartbeat was on par with an Alex Van Halen drum solo. "I don't mean to be like that," he said. "But...yeah, I've noticed you. If that's made you uncomfortable, I totally get it."

"It has," Charlie replied, "just not in the way that you think it is."

Russ smirked, "I'm confused," he said. "I'm not sure what you're saying."

Charlie matched Russ' smirk, "There's a thing with girls, when we're waiting for a guy to, well, make a move, initiate the first kiss, there's a bit of a frustration attached to it. The guy always seems to play it cool, wait too long, bide his time, that sort of thing. Even if we really like the guy, it tends to get a little bit, well, irritating."

"Can you blame us?" Russ asked. "It's nerve racking, especially in this day and age."

Charlie nodded, "I get it. And it's sweet. But if we like you, you should be able to see it pretty clearly."

Shaking his head, Russ admitted, "It's almost impossible to know sometimes. Girls are a bit...cryptic."

A laugh trickled out of Charlie's cupid bow-shaped lips, "I'll give you that... but if we're moving away from talking about things in a hypothetical sense, if we're talking about you and me," her cheeks flushed red, "I *do* like you, Russ. I just never thought you'd ever do anything about it."

The news was like music to Russ' ears. *No way*, his mind prattled. *I'm dreaming. This isn't happening. Even if it is, Charlie is just pulling one over on me.*

"Are you serious?" he asked.

Charlie laughed again, "I am, Russ. Every time you haven't been looking, I've looked at you, too. To be honest, I just thought you were maybe…*pretentious*, like you thought I was beneath you or something."

The whites of Russ' eyes were showing, "Are you kidding me?" he said with an incredulous tone. "I thought the same about you. Why would you think in a million years I thought I was better than you, or whatever?"

Charlie shrugged, "I read some of your writing."

The prospect of Charlie's eyes scanning *anything* that Russ wrote twisted his bowels into tight knots, "What do you mean?"

"A year ago," Charlie said, "we were in Honors English together. We had to write a short story and Ms. Rupe made everyone do a blind grading of each other's papers. Don't you remember? She ended up passing the papers out and all of us had to grade the other person's paper anonymously. I got your paper. You wrote the short story about a soldier who found out he had a daughter that he never knew about. Remember? He was blind."

A goofy smile radiated across Russ' face, "I had no idea. I mean, I remember you marking some syntax and structural errors, but you still gave me an A minus."

Charlie nodded, "I did," she said. "But it was the most interesting thing I read. It's clear what you're going to do later in life, Russ. You're *definitely* going to be a writer."

A cool breeze blew through. Russ stared deep into Charlie's eyes. She did the same. In that moment, he couldn't help but note how comfortable he felt in her presence, how easy it was to speak to her. So many times, he thought it would be close to impossible to have a conversation with her, that he'd stumble over his words or make her feel awkward—but that wasn't the case. It felt natural. He felt exactly where he needed to be.

"Charlie," Russ said, taking a small step forward. "I know this is so abrupt. I know that we only have like four days left in school. I know you're going to go away to school in the fall, and I'll be stuck here in LC. To be fair, I'm not sure anything would work between us because we're just starting our lives. But I'd regret it if I didn't ask if you maybe wanted to…hang out before all of that happens."

Beaming from one ear to the next, Charlie leaned in, kissed Russ on the cheek, and said, "Of course, I do. I'm just a little peeved it took you four years to ask."

Cloud nine didn't even get close to describing how Russ felt. Charlie waved goodbye—but not before plugging her number into his cell phone—went about her valedictorian duties as Russ, jazzed beyond belief, walked back to the car and informed Jacob as to what transpired.

***

Russ groaned, peeled his eyeglasses off, and deleted the section of the word document where he described being on cloud nine.

"Good lord, Russ," he said to himself, leaning back and shaking his head. "You've been doing this for fifteen years. You're better than that."

The door to Russ' office opened. His wife, Charlie, stood in the doorway with a steaming mug of coffee in her hands.

"It's so early," she said. "What are you doing up?"

Russ turned and smiled. "Just fooling around with a short story, hon," he said. "I've got two days before the editor gets the book back to me and we get into the marketing phase, so I just wanted to write something of my own."

Charlie, her eyes pinned Russ' monitor, said, "What are you writing?"

Closing the laptop, Russ said, "I'll let you read it when I fine tune it a bit. It's a bit messy."

Charlie placed down her mug and sat on her husband's lap. "Can you tell me what it's about?"

"Sure," Russ said. "It's about when I finally asked you out in High School. Some of it is a bit embellished but

I did it for sake of good fiction. It's not flowing right just yet. It still feels a bit...*impractical.* I'll also have to change the names, too, but it's about," he squinted, thinking it through, "75 percent accurate."

"How does it end?"

"It ends when I asked you out. I mean, I did it in the Starbucks back in LC, but I set it on the football field. I don't know. The visual of that just works better for some reason."

"I get it," Charlie said. "Is Jacob in the story?"

Russ nodded. "Big time. I wanted to write a bit at the end saying how he finally made a career in stand up."

Charlie said, "He called your cell phone about thirty minutes ago. I saw a missed call when I was making coffee."

"Yeah," Russ said. "His Netflix special is taping this Friday. He said he was going to get us tickets. He was probably calling about the details."

"That's great," Charlie said.

"What about visiting L.A. soon?" Russ asked curiously.

Charlie furrowed her brow. In the six years they lived in Chicago, Russ had never mentioned wanting to go back. "Really?" she said.

Russ nodded. "Jacob told me his sitcom is taping in the fall, and you're doing commencement speech for the new class at Cal Tech around the same time so the timeline works out well."

Charlie said, "You really want to go back there? You hated L.A., LC even more so."

Russ glanced at his computer. "I do," he said. "I wanted to go back to LC for sake of this story I'm writing.

I'm not sure if it will amount to anything, but I still want to go back."

"Up to you, babe." Charlie gestured to the monitor. "Tell me, how accurate is my character in this story?"

Smirking, Russ said, "Dr. Elliot…not one part of who you are in that story is fiction."

Leaning in close, Charlie planted a kiss on Russ' face and held it for as long as possible.

A KISS OF SEDUCTION – Part 1

1868

"Four men are missing," the Colonel told Hardwick. "Four of my *best* men. I sent them out on a week ago on a task and they never came back."

Captain Hardwick stood tall before his superior officer. He was only thirty years of age, but his time during the war that pitted brother against brother made others reason he was ten years older. His skin was slightly leathered. His cobalt-colored eyes possessed a patina that made them appear as though pieces of a razor were set into his pupils. Those who knew Hardwick swore he never blinked, never smiled, never showed any outward signs of emotion. He had his reasons.

"Captain," the Colonel said as he stood up from his desk, "you're set to be discharged next week, are you not?"

Hardwick nodded. "Yes, sir."

The Colonel lingered near the window, the expanse of the Arizona desert outside of it vast and unrelenting. The fervor outside had accumulated into unbearable temperatures and caused beads of sweat to gather on his brow. The Colonel dabbed at them with a handkerchief as he continued speaking.

"You've fought well for your country," he said. "You volunteered for missions that were, to put it simply, borderline suicidal. I'm surprised to find that you have survived as long as you have."

Hardwick said nothing.

"You have a rabbit's foot charm, son." The Colonel smirked. "Maybe God has an angel on your shoulder. Maybe he's let you live this long to see that you make it through this next assignment."

Finding four men who got lost in the desert?

Hardwick thought. *Hardly a taxing a chore.*

The Colonel moved to his desk. He sat down, unbuttoning the top of his navy-blue wool coat peppered with medals and patches. "I'll be frank with you," he said. "This task I'm requesting you to take part in is not as straight-forward as it may sound."

Request? He's making it a point to not say the word 'order.'

"Captain Hardwick," the Colonel said. "How much do you know about this area?"

Hardwick shook his head. "Not much, sir. I was transferred here a week ago. Most of my duties have been limited establishing protection details for the outposts that have been erected about 100 miles from here until I was requested to report to you this very morning."

The Colonel wagged a finger, "And you've done a damn fine job. After everything you went through on the frontlines, the assignment you were given out here was meant as a reprieve, was it not? Six years of charging into battle time after time, you were due for a change in pace."

Hardwick nodded. "Yes, sir."

"Tell me," the Colonel said, his had drifting toward Hardwick's file splayed out across his desk, "what type of pension are you looking at, son?"

Hardwick's eyes flickered. The conversation with the Colonel was becoming confusing at best. "Sir?" he asked.

"Be frank," the Colonel said. "All of these questions have a point."

Head held high, Hardwick said, "I've been given a small patch of land in Utah. I plan on raising cattle, sir. A modest living but a welcomed one nonetheless."

"You're being coy," the Colonel said. "You're being paid a meager salary upon your departure from the military. Quite honestly, I think it's a paltry sum compared to what I'm going to offer you for partaking in this endeavor."

The lines in Hardwick's brow furrowed, "I'm confused, sir. I was under the impression that this assignment was mandatory."

Shaking his head, the Colonel admitted, "It's not. This is a duty that will only be taken on should you agree to it. Again, I've been withholding certain details of this consignment, and should you take part in it, well, your compensation that you were already going to receive will be tripled upon completion of this undertaking."

The amount of money Hardwick was being promised would last him three lifetimes. "I see," he said.

"Then I am curious to know what exactly it is that you are asking me to do, sir."

The Colonel steepled his fingers. He sat back in his chair, a curious glint now in his eyes. "What are your thoughts on…superstitions, son? Tales of the unknown? Otherworldly encounters?"

Hardwick didn't believe in God. He sure as hell didn't believe in stories of ghost, ghouls, demons, or anything in league with stories to which only children gave any stock.

"I don't have any thoughts on them, sir," he said. "I find that it is a waste of time, putting it simply."

"As do I," the Colonel said. "Or at least I did, anyway. I've mentioned that four of my lieutenants have gone missing."

"You have."

"I didn't mention to you why I had sent them out to begin with. They were sent to detain someone who was alleged to have killed close to seven native children in a region designated as a temporary safe zone for a tribe that was pushed out of the area. The details of said crime are…ghastly, to say the least. Dismemberment. Molestation of the bodies. Things that one might attribute to the more savage of natives in this part of the country."

"I see," Hardwick said, the mentions of bodily harm and the grisly treatments of a corpse a simple fact of life for him after all he had seen and done.

"The men never returned," the Colonel said. "I can only speculate as to why. I sent a Corporal to scout the region in an attempt to find them. He returned two days later and informed me he ran into a group of natives twenty miles south of here. He left here a wide-eyed and optimistic man with aspirations of one day becoming a general, but he returned to me looking as though he'd seen a ghost. Apparently, this young man was told by this tribe that the group I sent was, in his words, 'torn apart piece by piece in a malicious and unspeakable manner.'"

Hardwick shrugged. "They might have encountered a resistance," he said dismissively. "And if I may I speak frankly…"

The Colonel nodded. "You may."

"Well," Hardwick continued, "perhaps your man was not cut out for the job. It sounds like he has a hard time discerning what is truth and what is nothing more than the common folklore of the natives."

"My thoughts exactly," The Colonel said. "There was also something else that this Corporal mentioned. He told me this tribe said there was…an entity in the area that was responsible not only for the death of the native children but for my men as well, a legend that goes by the name of

'Wendigo.' He claimed to have encountered this…*thing* during his return one evening in the wilderness."

Tales of native American folklore were ones with which Hardwick was well familiarized at this point in his career. Again, he gave no stock to it.

"I haven't heard of this particular legend, sir," he said. "But again, I see this as nothing more than a campfire tale being implement in lieu of said Corporal doing his job."

"Again," the Colonel said, "my thoughts were one-and-the-same. I assumed the Corporal was spinning yarn in light of the fact that he failed to fulfill his duties, so I sent him to the stockade for a night in a bid to sober up. My plan was to have him return to my quarters the next day to discuss what had transpired. When I informed him he was to spend the night reflecting on his failures in a cell, I had to have four men restrain him. The Corporal struggled and clawed his way through the men I assigned to detain him. When I asked why he was putting up such a fight, he insisted to me he had been cursed one night by this Wendigo fable during his alleged encounter, and that a mark was left on him for trespassing on this creature's grounds. I paid no mind to his rantings. The next morning, however," the Colonel drew a breath, "I found the Corporal ripped to pieces in his cell. Bit by bit. Piece by piece."

Hardwick said nothing.

"It wasn't any of my men," the Colonel said. "In fact, they claimed to have heard a beast, something akin to a cougar or bear or boar or, in one man's words, a combination of all three shrieking to high heaven during the night the Corporal spent in his cell. They ran to the cell to see what the commotion was all about, and that's when they found…what was left of the Corporal. They also claimed the door to the jail was locked, that nothing, that no one could have gotten inside."

The story made no sense to Hardwick. For a moment, he thought he wasn't hearing the Colonel correctly.

"Sir," he said, "this is quite a tale. I'm having a hard time following it."

"Understandable," the Colonel said. "And I spent the next two days questioning each of the men who were put in charge of keeping guard of the Corporal, some of the finest men I have ever known. Two of them haven't been able to speak since the ordeal. One of them may very well have gone inside. None of the details of this story line up." He shook his head. "I'm having a hard time grasping it myself."

Again, Hardwick said nothing.

"One of the men," the Colonel said, "claimed they saw the figure of a woman in the distance when they scoured the terrain for whatever was responsible. Perhaps it was a figment of his imagination, his mind attempting to make sense of the madness. It's a mess to say the least, Captain." He pointed to Hardwick. "And I want you to sort it out."

Nodding, Hardwick intoned, "I see."

The Colonel stood up. "I want you to find out what happened to my men," he said. "I want you to traverse the area where I sent them and find out what happened. I want to know if they're still alive, if they are merely lost and struggling to find their way back. If they have truly perished, then I want evidence of this brought back to me. You will have as much time as need be, and once again, your reward for this will be well worth the time."

"Why me, sir?" Hardwick inquired. "If I may ask."

"Because," the Colonel said, "you are a dutiful soldier of the highest possible caliber. You come highly recommended. And quite frankly," he shrugged, "no one else wishes to participate. Those who I've ordered to go have flat-out refused. Everyone is inclined to believe that this Wendigo story is true. I myself am not sure what to lend credit to. Knowing what I know about you, I'm prone to think you are of the mind that all of this mysticism and mythology, despite what you have just been told, is nothing more than fodder."

"I am," Hardwick agreed, "sir."

The Colonel nodded, "Then you are the best man for the job. If you agree, I will give you the details of where you will go, all the proper supplies, and anything else you may need. But the decision is yours and yours alone."

It took only a quick moment for Hardwick to agree. There were no cursed beasts padding their way through the desert. All that transpired was the result of the savagery of the natives. Having dispatched four of them during the course of his career, Hardwick was certain he could handle the assignment.

***

Hardwick entered the stables. A private who seemed unable to sprout hair on his face approached, reins in his hand and pulling a robust, carob-colored horse alongside him.

"His name's Buckley," the private said. "Loyal as loyal can be. The Colonel told me to give you the best horse we had on hand for your task."

Hardwick patted the animal's mane, "He'll do just fine." He gestured to the rifle and saddlebags filled with food, ammunition, a tent, and other supplies near the door. "Would you mind loading these up for me, Private?"

The private nodded, "Yes, sir."

Hardwick pulled the map out of his coat pocket given to him by the Colonel. Areas on the map were marked in red ink, a quarter-sized circle marked around a spot fifty miles to the north where the gaggle of men the Colonel had dispatched were last seen. Dusk was rapidly approaching. Hardwick wanted to cover at least twenty miles before setting up camp.

"You're ready," the private called out as he tightened the straps securing Hardwick's bags.

Hardwick folded the map and placed it back into his coat pocket, "Thank you, Private. Much obliged."

A quizzical look was fixed on the Private's face. "Sir," he said curiously, "can I ask you a question?"

"By all means," Hardwick said.

"You've heard about the stories, right? The ones about the men that the Colonel set out? The Corporal that lost his mind?"

Nodding, Hardwick affirmed, "I have."

"Are they true, sir?" the Private asked, his composure like one of a timid child. "Did those men really get torn to pieces by some kind of monster? Was the Corporal slaughtered by some kind of beast?"

"No," Hardwick said. "It's just campfire tales. You shouldn't be paying any mind to such nonsense."

The Private's expression was one of pure fear, his hands trembling as he jutted his chin toward the vast array of desert outside the stable doors. "I'm not much for superstition, sir," he said. "I've never been afraid of anything like ghosts or ghouls. But…there's been something strange brewing in the air around these parts. I can't quite put my finger on it, but it's like a sour scent clinging to everything."

The comment prompted Hardwick to tap two fingers against his skull. "It's your mind playing tricks on you, Private," he said. "All of the men in these parts have been privy to stories of death and mutilation for the past few days. When terrible things happen that don't make much sense, people like to make up fables to make them make sense, if you know what I mean."

The Private nodded, "I do, sir," he said. "But something is just plain off about this whole thing. I can't shake the feeling like…like I'm being watched."

The anxieties plaguing the young man meant nothing to Hardwick. He himself had not been much different at that same age. All it took was a war and becoming a witness to the death of so many good men to desensitize him. In many ways, he envied the Private.

"What's your name?" Hardwick asked him.

"Gibbons," the Private said.

"Well, Gibbons," Hardwick clapped his hand on the Private's shoulder, "all you need to worry about in this life is the fury of your fellow man. It is the only true evil that exists in this world. Put away childish notions of the boogeyman. That's fodder for children."

With that, Hardwick mounted his steed, patted its mane, and set out for his journey into the desert. He rode hard for the first twenty minutes of his trek until the horse, Buckley, required a brief rest. The gallop eased down into a slow trot, Hardwick taking a moment to assess the valleys and peaks covered in a rusted hue. Wildlife ranged from the occasional coyote to a scurrying lizard moving fast to stay ahead of the predatory hawks circling overhead. What became most curious to Hardwick was the further he distanced himself from the outpost, the more that the wildlife seem to dwindle, almost as if they were making it a point to steer clear of the area where the Colonel and the mentally unsound Corporal delving out stories of mythical creatures had informed Hardwick a slew of deaths had taken place.

***

Hardwick erected his tent in-between a pair of boulders in the middle of the desert, the nighttime chill having set in swiftly. The stark contrast between the unrelenting heat that had tormented Hardwick during his journey had shifted to a frosty temperature just as quickly as a man who was living became dead in an instant thanks to the simple pull of a gunman's trigger.

Hardwick turned his head toward the full moon above, the twinkling sea of stars vibrant and vast. The heat from the sizzling campfire warmed his face, Hardwick taking a sip of water from his canteen as Buckley proceeded to finish off the grain that his master had provided for him.

Buckley puttered his lips. The horse raised its head and looked pensively out toward the horizon, shifting his weight as though a predator was lingering close by.

Hardwick looked curiously at his steed. "What do you see, friend?"

The horse kept his focus glued to the darkness that enveloped the camp, the glow of Hardwick's fire illuminating only a small radius of the terrain.

"It's probably just a fox, fella," Hardwick said to the horse. "Don't let it get to you."

The wind blowing through camp intensified. Hardwick turned up the collars of his coat as the invisible gas licked at the fire repeatedly as though God himself was attempting to extinguish it. Hardwick thought nothing of it. He had been in more cumbersome situations in the wilderness before, and fear was no longer a part of his vernacular. Men didn't frighten him, creatures just the same.

Buckley stomped its hooves into the ground and then emitted a sound akin to that of a lite shriek. Hardwick stood, looking curiously at the horse before appraising the terrain.

That's when he saw a figure off in the distance.

Hardwick produced his six-shooter. He kept the weapon draped at his side, bellowing out to the figure, "Who goes there?"

The figure didn't move. What was peculiar to Hardwick was that, despite the tumultuous winds that were blowing, the clothing on the apparition didn't become tousled. The figure remained still. Completely placid. Almost as if it were a statue.

What is that? Hardwick thought. *Maybe it's my mind playing tricks on me.*

A KISS OF SEDUCTION – Part 2

***

Hardwick entered the mouth of the canyon. The walls were separated close to twenty feet. Meager slivers of light filtered in through the skies above, the clouds concealing the sun somber and weighty. Everything about the canyon felt unnatural, the angles appearing handmade. Hardwick had seen many things during his tenure as a soldier. He saw men butchered, droves of them slaughtered because of cannon fire or skewered to pieces by the tip of a bayonet. It desensitized him, made him a formidable man whose heart, one could argue, was made of stone. But something about the canyon, the irregular way it weaved and bent and spanned on for miles instilled him with a sickly impression.

Buckley slowed his pace, whinnying and attempting to turn back around. Hardwick tugged at the horse's reigns, furrowing his brow and curious as to what was spooking his animal.

"Easy, boy," he said. "Come on now. What's the problem?"

The horse's eyes widened. He puttered out something like that of a whimper and stomped his heels in the earth. No matter how hard Hardwick tried, the horse simply refused to move.

"Good God almighty," Hardwick groaned. "You're a stubborn S-O-B, aren't you?"

A jagged piece of rock fell from the top of the canyon. It tumbled down, rolling with significant momentum. Hardwick tracked the stone with his eyes, watching with a curious mind and feeling like the stone had a mind of its own. It skipped back and forth between the canyon walls until it settled on the ground—and then it tumbled and rolled straight in Hardwick's direction.

Buckley bawled. He sprung hard and threw up its front legs. Hardwick attempted to control the animal as best he could, but when the horse bucked a second time, Hardwick was thrown off its back. He landed on his side, the air feeling like it had been knocked clean out of his lungs. He turned over, swiping his hand and Buckley's reigns but to no avail. The horse was fleeing as far and fast as it could from the canyon.

Hardwick's breathing was shallow. The effort it took to pull air into his lungs was a cumbersome ordeal. As soon as his breaths returned to a steady and standard rhythm, he stood up, brushed the dirt from his trousers, and saw that Buckley had turned into a faint outline in the distance.

All my supplies were with him, he thought. *Everything.*

Normal men would have cursed to high heaven, stamped their feet into the ground, and turned their head toward the sky to utter obscenities at God for the bad stroke of luck—but not Hardwick. Even before the war, during the times he was just a child, he had experienced more pain, sorrow, and bad luck than any juvenile should ever have to experience. It seasoned him, weathered him to the point that something like Buckley running off with three days' worth of food and the repeater rifle strapped to the saddle was but a minor inconvenience.

I still have my pistol, Hardwick told himself before grazing his hand across the cold steel attached to his hip. *Those natives will probably run into Buckley most likely. I'll get that brute back. I still can't understand what spooked him.*

Hardwick turned to lay eyes on the stone that had skidded down the canyon walls—but it was gone. For a moment, he felt light-headed, a feeling overcoming him like he was living in a dream.

He ogled the canyon walls. "Why did I come here?" he asked himself. He was far off the beaten path, well off the preplanned route he had intended to take in a bid to locate the missing men the Colonel sent him after. But something about the canyon drew him to enter. Hardwick couldn't explain it. It was as though the canyon were a magnet and Hardwick were comprised entirely of metal.

He slowly padded his way through the canyon. A cold breeze wafted through and rose the hairs on the back of his neck. The closer he descended into the belly of the chasm; the more Hardwick felt like an unseen party was watching him closely. He withdrew the six-shooter from his holster, holding it tightly in his hand and resolved to shoot first and ask questions later.

"Michael."

Hardwick stopped in his tracks. He raised his weapon and quickly cocked back the hammer. No one had referred to him by his Christian name in years. The last person who did was his mother who cried out his name from the family home before the inferno that consumed it caused it to buckle in on itself and collapse to the ground— and whoever had just called out his name sounded unerringly like her.

"Show yourself," Hardwick said. "Unless you want a stomach full of a lead, I'd suggest you quit playing around."

Silence held sway. The breeze gusting through abruptly ceased. Hardwick began to train his weapon from left to right, sweeping it and caressing the trigger with his finger.

"*Michael*," the voice called out again. "My sweet Michael…"

Hardwick's heart raced. *That's my mother's voice,* his mind prattled. *That's her*!

He parted his lips. It felt as though all the moisture in his mouth had evaporated in the blink of an eye. He cleared his throat, scrutinizing every inch of the valley in a bid to find the location of whoever was calling out his name.

Maybe I'm dreaming, he thought. *Maybe I was knocked unconscious. Maybe I'm lying back on a bed at the fort being tended to by a nurse and this is nothing more than the product of a fever taking over my mind.*

"Michael," the voice called out again. "Don't you remember me?"

The sound of his mother's accent calling out to Hardwick enraged him. "*Enough!*" he shouted. "I'm going to start shooting. Show yourself. Now!"

The sounds of feet shuffling across the ground ahead of Hardwick was like a faint scratching. He had his fill of the toying around. He raised his pistol and fired off a shot into the darkness. And then another. And then another.

The crack of the shot reverberated through the canyon walls. Hardwick kept his gaze peeled, looking for signs of a body.

"Michael," his mother's voice beckoned. "You don't want to hurt me. I'm your mother. I brought you into the world."

It's not her, he told himself. *I must be losing my mind.*

"You're not my mother," he called back.

The voice began to hum a melody. Hardwick recognized it immediately. After a moment, the humming turned into singing.

"My sweet boy," his mother crooned, "my only sweet boy…I'll love you always…you bring me such joy…"

"Stop," Hardwick whispered. "Please, stop…"

The voice was closer. Darkness began to envelope Hardwick. He felt the hairs on the back of his neck stand up, his hand trembling, the air feeling like it was being snatched out of his lungs.

"My sweet boy," his mother said, Hardwick feeling her presence just an arm's reach away, "come with me…*my sweet boy.*"

Hardwick felt a searing sensation spread across his chest. He was knocked onto his back, Hardwick gasping as his pistol scattered across the ground. Darkness consumed the canyon. Hardwick couldn't make out a single thing.

His nostrils turned up. Hardwick picked up on a foul odor that stung his eyes and forced him to cover his face with his hand. The voice of his mother changed to something closer to a baritone level, the voice raspy like it had been thrashed apart by razorblades.

"*Go,*" the voice said. "Leave before it's too late."

Hardwick felt a kick make contact with his ribs. It felt like a hoof had made contact with his torso, something that he had experienced several times before.

"Go," the voice repeated. "Go and never come back."

The stench dissipated. Light returned to the canyon. Hardwick pulled air deep into his lungs, stoop up, and took a look around. His hand hovered near his jacket pocket. A warmness began to radiate across his chest. Hardwick quickly patted himself down, worried that he had sustained some kind of injury. Upon reaching into his jacket, his hand grazed the ruby stone that the Native boy had given him.

Why is it so warm? he thought

Hardwick pulled out the stone to find that it was glowing subtly. He blinked several times, concerned that his eyes were simply playing tricks on him—but they weren't. The stone was glowing, and a hiss emanated from several yards away like the shrieking of a panicked animal.

***

Night had fallen. Hardwick set up camp inside of the ravine. For several hours, his mind had been replaying the events from earlier that day. No matter how hard he tried to convince himself that it was all a dream, the facts pointed to the case that it was not.

It happened, he told himself. *You've wandered into some kind of treacherous territory here, the home of some kind of mythical beast.*

He shook his head. The notion that the stories pertaining to the Wendigo being told in truth sent a shiver up his spine.

"This can't be happening," he said. "I can't believe this is real."

What was it? he pondered. *Could ghosts exists? If they do, could angels? Demons? God? Heaven?*

Thoughts of the afterlife or a higher power reigning supreme over the human race was something Hardwick had dismissed a long time ago. So much death had plagued his life, so much strife, and endless amount of turmoil. All the war. All the struggle. The death of his mother...

His eyes widened. *Was it possible,* he wondered, *if that was my mother? It can't be...but if it wasn't, that meant this...creature was playing tricks on me. It* knew *about my mother. That means that it somehow has the ability to...read my mind.*

Hardwick's hand trembled. It hadn't done so in years. He flexed his grip and turned his head toward the night sky. The black canvas of sky was peppered with twinkling stars. Hardwick counted the hours he had been

awake and figured it was most likely ten or eleven at night.

He wanted to continue his trek to find the lost men.

Wendigo or not, he would not be scared away. He had a

duty to fulfill, and nothing would get in his way.

Turning up the collar of his coat, Hardwick then

lied on his side. He crossed his arms and counted his

breaths, drawing in air slowly and then releasing it. He did

this several times until his eyelids fluttered, his muscles

slackened, and sleep overcame him in a glorious wave.

***

Hardwick opened his eyes to find himself standing

in a field of golden wheat. His eyes scanned the terrain.

The fields seemed to span on into eternity. Glancing up at

the bright blue skies overhead, he felt the sense that he was

in an area he was not familiar with, and he had travelled to

most parts of the states at this point in his life.

He reached out his hands. They were free of grime or the scars he had sustained during his time in battle. He was dressed in overalls, the same ones he wore back when he was a young man. Hardwick ran his hand across his face. It was free of stubble, smooth like it was before he was able to sprout hair.

"Darling," his mother called out. "Look at me."

Hardwick turned around. A warm sensation filled his sternum. His heart felt full as he laid eyes on his mother. She smiled warmly at him, wearing the same flaxen-colored prairie dress she did when she was still alive. There was a glow about her, the same kind that the sun gave off when it was reflected across water.

"Mother?" Hardwick said. "Is that really you?"

She nodded. "Yes, my dear," she cooed. "Do you know where you are?"

Hardwick ogled the grain that surrounded him. "I don't," he said. "I've never seen this place before."

His mother's smiled broadened. "You will someday," she assured him. "Not for a long time, but you will. Your entire family is here, my love. They are watching over you as we speak."

Hardwick glanced around. "I don't see them."

She crooked her finger toward the sky. "They are watching," she said. "Trust me when I tell you that they are. This is a place of safety, one in which there is no pain. No fear. No turmoil or strife. All is well in this haven. The sun is always shining. The wind is always blowing."

He inched closer to his mother. "I feel at peace," he said. "I have not felt this way in quite some time."

She outstretched her arms. "Come here, my dear," she said.

Hardwick walked briskly toward his mother and wrapped his arms around her. He was surprised to find that he stood just above her waist like he did when he was a boy.

"I'm confused, mother," he said. "I don't know what's happening."

"It will all make sense in time," she said.

"Was that you?" he asked. "Was that you that I heard today? Was it you that I saw?"

His mother cupped her hands around his face. "Listen to me, my boy," she said. "What you saw, what you heard today was a trick. You were not speaking to me. You were speaking to an otherworldly creature. It has the ability to look into your soul, to know who you are and to use that against you."

Hardwick closed his eyes. "So, it's true," he said. "The stories I was told about that...*creature* are true."

She nodded. "I'm afraid they are, my dear. This…entity is attempting to lure you in, to lower your defenses."

"Why?" he asked. "What could it possibly want with me?"

His mother drew a shaky breath. "It wants your *soul*, my son," she said. "It feeds on the pain of others. It uses the things you know and hold dear to your heart in a bid to defeat you. It has done this for centuries. I have been watching it close in on you from the place we are in now. I've watched desperately as I've prayed witness to my only son being preyed upon by a monster."

Hardwick shook his head. He then looked deep into his mother's eyes. "I have lived long," he said. "I have seen much. I have learned to not be fearful of any man who I have crossed paths with. But this…*thing*, this creature is different. I feel as vulnerable as I did when I was a child."

She nodded. "That is its plan," she said. "It knows this about you. The stronger the person it preys upon, the more it can feed off of them once it has lowered their defenses. It wants you desperately, my boy. It lusts after you more that it has any other."

"Then I should leave," he said. "I should go back before a fate befalls me like it did the other men."

"You cannot do that," his mother pleaded. "This creature has plagued these lands long before the first man walked the earth. It will never stop. It will continue to bring pain to others long after you are gone. Only you can defeat it, my darling. You must be strong. You must bring an end to the reign of terror that this beast has brought upon the earth."

"How?" Hardwick asked. "What do I do, mother?"

His mother held out a fist. She slowly opened it to reveal the same ruby-colored stone that the Native boy had gifted to Hardwick.

"Use what you have been given," she said. "Trap the creature in this stone. Lure him in. Use his tactics against him. But you must be mindful. It will do what it can to trick you. It will make you believe it is something it is not. Once it has convinced you of this, it will destroy you. It will seduce you with a simple kiss and then end your life in the most heinous of ways."

Hardwick took the stone from his mother. "How do I use it?" he asked. "How does it work?"

"The creature must eat it," she instructed. "It must devour the stone like it devours its prey."

"That's impossible," Hardwick said. "How would I ever pull off such a feat?"

Smiling once more, his mother slowly backed away. "In time, you will know," she said. "Be strong, my son. It is not your time to join your family in this place. You must live. You must do what you have been placed on this earth to do. Be well, my darling. Be safe."

Hardwick watched as his mother walked away into the distance. He reached out his hand, hoping she would stay, desperate to fill the time that he had lost after she was taken from him prematurely as a child.

"No, mother!" he pleaded. "Please, stay. Stay with me!"

His mother waved goodbye. Hardwick ran toward her. He then felt as though the ground beneath him had vanished, his body weightless as the light ceased and darkness overcame him.

***

Hardwick's eyes shot open. His breathing was shallow. Perspiration clung to his brow. He ogled his surroundings and saw that he was back in the ravine, the stars still shining overhead. He could still pick up on his mother's scent clinging to his clothing.

That was her, he told himself. *I could feel her presence. That was no trick of the mind.*

He reached into his coat and produced the stone, the tales that his mother told him about the Wendigo playing back in his mind.

"You must live," he could hear his mother say. "You must do what you have been placed on this earth to do."

Hardwick drew a deep breath. He pocketed the stone, stood up, grabbed his pistol, and stuffed it into his holster. He was fearful beyond measure, panicked more than he ever had been in his life. He did not want to confront the beast—but he could not live with knowing that his mother, living now in a place he thought was nothing more than a fable, was disappointed with him not fulfilling what she referred to as his "duty." With that, Hardwick held his head high, turned his head to the left, and saw that the canyon walls narrowed and led to the mouth of a cave.

***

The opening to the cave was narrow, enough space that Hardwick could squeeze in his body but not much more. A sulfuric odor was in the air, a stench that seemed comprised of filth, rot, and decay.

"This is it's home," he whispered. "This is where the Wendigo dwells."

He puffed his chest and double-checked that the stone was in his pocket. Hardwick then removed the pistol, entered the cave, and saw a cramped passageway that led deep into the belly of darkness. He took his first step inside, a hot gust of air then lapping him in the face. The stench was unbearable, infinitely worse than the decomposition that Hardwick had smelled on the fields of battle.

"Go back," a hiss-laced voice whispered. "I will not tell you again."

Don't be fearful, Hardwick, he told himself. *Fulfill your duty. Face this creature and find your way back home.*

He continued his ascent; the walls narrow and slick. Hardwick touched the rocks and found a thin layer of grime upon them. It seemed as though an eternity passed as he continued his journey into the belly of a cave.

"I'll hurt you," the hissing voice said. "I'll tear you apart limb by limb."

Keep going, Hardwick's mind prattled.

"I'll eat you," the voice said. "I'll destroy you."

Do not back down.

"I'll make you hurt. I'll make you bleed."

Hardwick saw the opening to a cavern. *You are almost there.*

"Last chance," the voice said. "Go now before you suffer greatly."

Hardwick took his last step into the cavern and found himself in a place the size of a small cathedral. The ceiling reached a good one-hundred feet above his head. The ground was open on all sides. It felt like a stone had been carved into a bowl-like shape—and standing in the center of it was a shadow.

"It's you," he said. "I know that you're there."

The shadow crooked a finger toward Hardwick's gun. "That is of no use to you," it grumbled.

Hardwick nodded. "I gathered as much."

"You are brave, young man," the shadow said. "Brave but foolish. It is like a, how do you phrase it, *marinade* that seeps into your skin. It will make my devouring of you all the sweeter."

Hardwick stopped and held his head high. "I'm not afraid of you," he said. "I will not give into your attempts at striking fear into me."

The shadow said nothing. A moment later, it slipped backward into the darkness. Silence held sway. A moment later, Hardwick heard the voice of his mother.

"My dear boy," she said. "That dream you had last night was not real. That was not me. That was simply a figment of your imagination."

Hardwick squeezed his eyes shut. "Don't listen to it," he thought. "It's trying to—"

"I'm not trying to trick you," his mother cut it. "I am here to save you. I am not the beast. I am an angel, sent from heaven to see that my boy is taken care of…"

His mother emerged from the darkness. She sported the same prairie dress and smile that Hardwick had seen in his dreams. She walked toward him, her scent overtaking the pungent aroma in the cavern.

"Come," she said. "Take my hand. Let me kiss your cheek and make everything better again."

Hardwick shook his head. "It's a trick," he said. "I was warned of your deception."

His mother inched closer, just a few paces away, her hands reaching out and her smile widening. "Kiss me, child," she said. "Come take your place by my side."

Hardwick felt defenseless. The air felt like it was being snatched from his lungs. He felt himself giving into his "mother's," commands, his lips parting in a bid to kiss his mother hello on the cheek.

"That's it," she said, his mother then reaching out her hand and placing it in Hardwick's. *"Come…"*

Hardwick took his mother's hand. She turned her face and leaned in for a kiss.

"*Don't!*" Hardwick heard his *true* mother say in his ear. "Don't give in!"

Hardwick stood back. He swatted away his false mother's hand, reached into his pocket, and pulled out the ruby stone. It began to glow, the figment before him now scowling.

"You're not my mother," Hardwick said. "You're nothing more than a trickster with a foul stench."

His false mother's shoulders slackened. The lines in her face turned down into a grimace. Its skin turned ashen gray, cracks forming like those in the terrain outside the cavern. Her fingernails grew into blade-like talons. The unbearable stench Hardwick picked up on before had returned.

"You *fool*," the beasts said, its teeth yellow and caked with blood. "I warned you."

Hardwick held out the stone—and then the creature rushed forward and dug its talons into his flesh. Hardwick emitted a shriek, the creature picking him up off the ground, its breath lapping at Hardwick and slapping him in the face.

"You are," it said, "by far the most delicious specimen I will ever have the pleasure of eating. Those men of yours will taste like pale slop in comparison…"

The pain in Hardwick's flesh felt like a million hot pokers began stuck into his body. The ruby stone, still clutched in his hand, turned a bright shade of white.

"Trick it!" he heard his mother say. "Use its tactics against itself!"

Hardwick was at a loss. The only thing he could think to do was stare the creature in its eyes that had turned a shade of blood red, grit his teeth, and say, "I am not Hardwick."

The creature cocked its head curiously and smirked. "What did you say, little man?"

"I-I," Hardwick stammered, "am an angel sent from heaven, you unsightly *fool*. I have come here to trick you. I have fooled you into thinking that I am someone I am not."

"*Laugh*," his mother said. "Continue to trick him!"

Despite the copious pain registering in his mind, Hardwick pulled back his lips and laughed. "You are mine," he said. "I have bested you."

The creature shook his head. "It is not possible," it said. "You lie to me!"

Hardwick inched his face closer. "I am the avenging hand of *God*," he said. "I have followed you, tracked you, have been dispatched by the man in the sky to do away with you once and for all."

The creature winced. It shuddered. It dropped Hardwick to the earth and began covering its ears. "Lies!" it said. "These are all *lies!*"

Hardwick looked at his hand gripping onto the stone. It levitated from his grip. He watched as the creature, falling onto its knees, bellowed out a pain-induced shriek.

The glowing stone was in front of the creature's agape mouth, the mouth widening to an unnatural state as the stone spun in place.

"Now!" Hardwick's mother cried. "Do it, now!"

Hardwick stood. He balled up his fist. He then threw it into the stone and watched as it violently entered the creature's mouth. The creature's eyes shot open. Heavenly light began to seep through the cracks in it skin.

"No!" it cried. "No! No! No!"

The light pouring out of the creature was like a stream of water, the harshness of the light so bright that

Hardwick was forced to cover his eyes. He turned away, the creature emitting a guttural shriek before it threw out its arms and an explosion of light filled the cave.

***

Lieutenant Reece Edmunds approached the cavern on horseback. It had been two days since the Colonel dispatched him to find Hardwick after he failed to return, the second party sent in a bid to find the lost gaggle of soldiers.

Something caught Edmund's attention off in the distance—a blurry figure. He hopped off of his saddle, raising his hand to his eyes and squinting in a bid to make out what he was seeing.

"Hello, there!" he shouted. "Who is that I'm looking at?"

The figure came in closer. Edmunds was stunned to find a disheveled Hardwick, his clothes ripped and tattered, and face covered in grime, approaching Edmunds with a depleted look on his face.

"Son of a gun," Edmunds whispered. He rushed toward Hardwick, clapping the man on his shoulders and asking if he was alright.

Hardwick nodded. "I am now."

"Where have you been?" Edmunds asked. "Where are the missing men you were sent to find?"

"They're gone," Hardwick said. "They were killed."

Edmunds sighed. "*Damn*," he said. "What happened to you? Your horse? Your supplies?"

"It's a long story," Hardwick said, appraising the wounds the creature had made and finding that they were no longer there.

Was it real? he thought. *Was I dreaming?*

"I'll take you back to the fort," Edmunds said. "We'll get you cleaned up and get a hot meal in your belly."

Hardwick nodded. "Much obliged."

Edmunds told Hardwick they could trade off riding the horse. After a few moments of riding, Edmunds asked what had happened.

"I'll tell you later," Hardwick said. "I'm still coming to terms with it myself."

Edmunds huffed. "Sounds like a rough night," he said. "I'm just glad that you're in one piece."

"*Son*," Hardwick could hear his mother say from the sky. He turned his head, the clouds ripe and plentiful, a glorious streak of light beaming down from the sky.

Yes, mother? he thought.

"Be happy," she told him. "Be free. We will see you when the time comes?"

Edmunds said, "Is everything alright, sir?"

Hardwick smiled. "I think it will be, friend," he said. "I think it will."

A KISS OF REVENGE

Flashback – 1990

Kelly, the quiet, shy, bookworm, was crushing hard on Steve, the oh-so-popular high school quarterback. Steve, of course, was in love, or more likely lust, with the head cheerleader, as the story often goes. How Kelly had come to find herself in this predicament was not unexpected.

Steve sat in front of her in Spanish class, where Señor Moore had placed his students in an effort to avoid the usual drama of high school cliques and promote greater learning. All in all, Señor Moore had seen his plan work each year and thus far, this year appeared to be no different. The class was on track to attend the annual foreign language competition in the capitol with everyone in this third year class participating.

Students were scheduled to do poetic readings, a play, a comedic skit, songs, and more. Señor Moore had asked for volunteers first, when they didn't come as quickly as he'd hoped, he began assigning roles.

"Esteban," Señor Moore began as he assigned the lead male role in the Spanish play they had been reading in class.

Kelly heard Steve say, *"Claro"* when asked. He sounded so confident with his "sure thing" – there was no hesitation at all.

Next, she heard her name called. She heard her own mind screaming, *"Noooooo wayyyyyyy!"* at exact moment her voice betrayed her with a simple, softspoken, *"Sí, Señor."*

And so, Kelly found herself cast in the play as the lead opposite Steve. She couldn't have been more shocked.

Panic set in as her mind raced, *"I can't do a play with Steve. We barely know each other. Sure, we've spoken in class – duh – he sits right in front of me. But, a play, I can't do a play. All those people watching. What if I screw it all up – the whole class will see, the whole school will know. I need to find a way out…"*

"Kelly?" Steve interrupted her racing thoughts, "You want to figure out a time when we can practice our lines? I know Señor Moore said we'd have plenty of time in class, but we have the most lines, so ya' know, we probably should practice outside of class."

"Say something," her mind instructed. "Yes…I guess we should…but don't you have practice?"

"Uh…football season is over and baseball practice hasn't started yet and I can do my workouts anytime. How about Thursday? Señor Moore said we could use the room after school."

"Good God he's all over this. How am I going to get out of it now? Has he always been so good-looking?" Kelly shut out her thoughts and answered, "Okay, Thursday then." As he walked away, she was finally able to take a deep breath, *"Now what am I going to do?"* she asked herself.

~~~~~~~~~

Kelly met Steve and Señor Moore the following Thursday. Mr. Moore wanted to guide their first solo practice to make sure they were getting the parts right – it was after all a tragic love story. Their first practice was awkward to say the least. Kelly felt ill-at-ease playing opposite Steve because in her mind they were opposites. Steve was good-looking, confident, self-assured. Kelly felt ordinary, shy, and insecure in his presence. Both he and Mr. Moore worked to get her to relax and have fun, but for Kelly, knowing 50 percent of her grade was riding on this had her even more stressed.

For Steve, the weightiness of the play on his grade was equally significant. Spanish came fairly easy to him unlike some other subjects and his GPA could use the boost, especially as college recruiters looked at his performance on the field and in the classroom. He knew Kelly was smart, he'd seen her in class, now all he had to do was get her to calm down and they could knock this competition out of the park. *"An excellent grade and an award from the prestigious foreign language competition would do wonders for his reputation among colleges. Hell, they might even fight over him which could mean a full scholarship to play football!"* His mind wandered before hearing Mr. Moore say his name.

"Kelly, you've got this! You know the language as well as anyone in class, including Steve. It's the reason I picked the two of you as the leads, you both have an ear for Spanish."

She smiled, thinking, *"Maybe I can do this?"* then added out loud, "Okay, let's try it again."

Steve winked at her, agreeing, "Let's do this."

While she didn't know what to do with the wink, after the pep talk with Mr. Moore, she felt more calm, more confident.

~~~~~~~~

They practiced every Thursday, as well as frequently in class with the other players. Steve was always patient and kind to Kelly. For the first time in his life, he found himself thinking he might be able to be friends with a girl.

As the time drew near for the competition, Kelly was feeling more confident. She actually found she was getting more comfortable in her own skin. She knew the lines to the play and only needed to work on her acting skills. It was hard for her to open up and play the role with the desired aplomb. Everyone encouraged her, particularly Steve, who she believed was becoming a friend.

They still had not practiced the final scene which closed with a kiss. It was just a simple kiss to close the show but Kelly was terrified. First of all, she had never been kissed. Second, she was afraid she was getting too close to Steve. He was part of the upper echelon of their high school, the "populars" and the "jocks." She was at best a mere "brainiac" and at worst a "normal."

Steve continued to be kind and encouraging to Kelly and all the other actors who would be performing with them in the upcoming play. He would even say he had become friends with some unexpected individuals in his Spanish class. There was Kelly, certainly one of "the brains" but there was also Mike "the floater" as well as Ruben and Connie, who were among the "hipsters" and "good-ats" respectively. Foreign language classes seemed to bring the classic cliques together in unexpected ways. Steve liked these new "friends," but he was wary what his girlfriend Macy might say.

Macy was beautiful, poised, well-spoken, definitely one of "the populars" and the head cheerleader to boot. Even so, Steve knew she coveted her place in the hierarchy of high school and expected him to do the same. He had told her about the play. She wasn't surprised, she was going to the competition too, and preparing a recitation of French poetry. They both could do with a GAP boost. What Steve hadn't told Macy was about his budding friendship with Kelly, Mike, Connie, Ruben, or the others in the play.

In the two week prior to their trip to the capitol for the competition, Steve, Kelly, and the rest of the cast worked on costumes, some minimalist sets, and of course their performances nearly every day. They had all been out together for burgers several times when practices and preparation had gone late. Steve and Kelly, whose parts were much larger, had met for extra practices at Kelly's favorite taco joint as well. The entire group had grown closer as they worked, practiced, and laughed together.

Kelly and Steve had agreed not to practice "the kiss" even before Señor Moore told them about a "stage kiss." He explained the fake kiss, in which Steve would place his hand on the side of Kelly's neck, his fingers behind her ear and thumb on her lips. They both agreed it was the ideal approach especially since Steve had a girlfriend.

The problem was no one had bothered to tell them, they might actually want to kiss by the time the performance arrived. Steve had kissed many girls over his teenage years, but he could not remember having ever kissed a cute brainiac like Kelly. He was genuinely curious and since it was a play it would give him an excellent excuse should Macy be concerned.

Kelly wanted to kiss Steve, not only because she was curious never having been kissed before, but because she was in the throes of a full-blown crush. She hadn't

wanted to fall for him, but she did and hard. She did her

best not to let it show. She thought of Steve as a friend and

didn't believe he could be more to her. Plus, she knew

Macy as one of the "mean girls" and truly didn't want to

cross her.

~~~~~~~

The parking lot was abuzz with activity as the

foreign language students boarded the buses headed for the

capitol. The teachers and chaperones had decided it best to

keep the respective classes together for the trip, making it

easier on arrival for each group to be at their competitions

on time and ready to go.

Kelly and Steve sat together surrounded by the

other players, hoping to get in a bit of additional practice on

the way. Their intentions, while good soon succumbed to

fits of laughter as they purposely flubbed their lines for laughs. Mr. Moore smiled, it was exactly what he'd hoped to see when he assigned the parts in the beginning.

On their arrival at the competition, Kelly Anne Stowe and Steven Ryan Cassidy, together with their cast of actors were ushered by Mr. Moore to their places. Each segment of the competition was held in separate buildings, Spanish in one, French in another, German in yet another, and so on. Once students had completed their performances, they were permitted to visit other buildings to cheer on their fellow classmates.

When the time came, Steve, Kelly, and the others donned their costumes, put their minimal props in place, and readied themselves. The play went off as a complete success, everyone played their parts perfectly and not a single line was missed. There was but a single surprise, when Steve issued his final line, *"En un beso, sabrás todo lo que he callado[1]"* he ditched the stage kiss and went in for a real one. Surprised as she was, Kelly kissed him back!

The audience erupted in a symphony of "ohs and ahs" and then offered the actors a standing ovation. Everyone took their bows and quickly exited the stage for the next group.

Steve led Kelly into an alcove backstage apparently hoping for a repeat performance, but Kelly stopped him. Yes, she had momentarily lost control of her senses, but quickly regained them as the audience reacted, "What are you doing?" she scolded, "Have you forgotten about Macy?"

He stopped short, never having expected her to call him on it, but rather expecting her to fall into his arms for additional kisses. She was exceptionally good at it but had

---

[1] In a kiss, you will know everything that I have kept quiet

no idea, and he wanted another taste, "Well..." he began just as Mr. Moore found them.

"Everything okay here?" he asked.

"*Sí, Señor,*" they answered in unison.

"We need everyone back out into the audience, it's almost time for the awards ceremony. Everyone will be joining us here for it."

Unable to continue their conversation, they headed with the rest of the cast out to the audience to watch the final performers and wait for the awards. Steve pulled Kelly into the seat beside him, just as Macy walked in with a group of French students and caught his eye.

He found himself in a conundrum. Macy was hot, but there was something about Kelly.

As the awards were announced, Señor Moore's unlikely group of players won first prize for their performance. Steve and Kelly, as the leads, were called on to accept the award for the group.

Even though Steve was oblivious, others had noticed Kelly's obvious crush, including Macy, but no one had discussed it simply because no one believed it would go anywhere. Kelly was Kelly, Macy was Macy, and well, Steve was Steve. Macy had been willing to ignore it until word reached her of the play-ending kiss.

The teenagers had been granted permission to ride the bus of their choosing home from the competition once they checked in with their teacher. Macy felt the gathering of a large number of the student body would be the ideal time to test Steve's loyalties while putting Kelly in her place. She kissed Steve and grabbed his hand, then called out, "Kelly, great performance today, especially while getting your first kiss from your first crush. You aim big, Girl!"

Steve, taken aback by the comment, had to act fast to maintain his reputation, so he laughed at Macy's words, put his arm around her, and walked away.

Kelly was mortified as nearly the entire senior class had heard Macy's hurtful comments. Worst of all, Steve had looked at her and then laughed at her before he strode away with Macy in his arms. It was the worst kind of humiliation, especially since every word Macy had said was true, but crueler still because she had believed Steve was her friend.

~~~~~~~~

Flash Forward - 2010

Anne Davidson was the toast of Hollywood. Her success as a director was legendary. She had worked hard earning her Bachelor of Fine Arts and later her Master of

Fine Arts, determined to overcome her painful past. While it seemed she had risen quickly to fame, the truth was her early years had been anything but filled with fame.

After a short stint, only one play, of acting in high school, she knew the limelight of center stage was not for her, but she loved being behind the scenes and helping to create a successful production. She began doing so in local productions during her university years and finally made her had made her directorial debut Off-Off Broadway. It was hard work, much harder than she expected.

Falling in love with one of the actors didn't help her career. Trey Davidson had the looks and charm and came on to her hard. She resisted at first, simply because he reminded her of someone she once knew, but finally he wore her down and she succumbed to his charms. Soon after they married and at first it was pure bliss. Then, Tray got his big break. It seemed theater productions were just too much work for him, so he decided they should flee the East Coast and head to Hollywood so they could make their mark. At least that was what he said. She agreed.

At first, they struggled together to make a name for themselves, but when his big break came first, he decided it was time to cash Anne in for his new co-star. Betrayed again, Anne became even more determined to succeed and so she did.

After a string of directing successes, Trey sought to reconnect, but was quickly rebuffed. Her career was on the rise and his had stalled, but Anne had decided if and when she fell in love again, she would be sure her paramour was in it for the long haul. As determined as she was to succeed, she was even more committed to guarding her heart.

Her latest project was a football movie with a murder mystery angle. The plot twists in the screenplay had been such a unique mix of genres, she decided to give it a try. She loved a challenge and believed she could make the movie a success.

Much to her surprise, when she met with the pre-production , she discovered Trey was being considered for one of the supporting roles.

"We'll see," she thought as the discussion continued.

Rick, the producer droned on about hiring a football consultant to make sure they got the nuances of the game right, and Anne nodded in agreement. "He's new to Hollywood, but comes highly recommended for his knowledge of the sport, Steve someone, I think, he had an

exceptional college career, but fizzled out in the NFL…"
Rick continued.

Anne listened to the remainder of the conversation, which ended with her first assistant director and the production manager making a plan to schedule screen tests for the actors and interviews for the proposed consultants.

~~~~~~~~

With the actors selected, Anne and Rick talked while waiting for the first interview with the potential consultants. Anne glanced at the list of scheduled interviewees and then she saw it – Steve R. Cassidy, consultant. *"It couldn't be!"* her mind reeled. *"If it is, things were going to get interesting really fast this morning,"* she pondered.

Rick noticed her rapt attention to the list, "What's up, Anne?" he queried.

"Nothing really, hey, what do you know about this Steve guy?"

"Not much, he was a pretty big deal in college, was drafted to the NFL, but then after a few years his career fizzled. He's worked on a couple of TV shows consulting on football, but this would be his first movie. From what I gather, he knows football, but I've also heard he can be a cocky jock, you know one of those guys who lives in his own "glory days."

They were interrupted by the production assistant before Rick could ask her why she was so curious, "Mr. Cassidy is here to see you," she stated.

Rick stood to greet him, "Steve, welcome, nice to meet you, this is our director, Anne Davidson."

Hello Steve, is it okay if I call you Steve? Anne asked trying to keep her thoughts under control. *"Damn, if it isn't Steve from high school"* she thought.

"Ms. Davidson, a pleasure to meet you," he turned on the charm but showed no glimmer of recollection.

Rick began the interview, but Anne was only half listening. She recognized Steve immediately, same as high school, cocky as hell, still thinking he was God's gift to women. She had tried, but had never forgotten the humiliation he had caused her in high school and seeing him today brought it all back, with a vengeance.

She watched him, joining in the conversation as needed, to see if he really recognized her and was simply faking it. Granted, her name was different and she looked nothing like the bookworm she had been in high school. In college, brainiac Kelly Anne Stowe had blossomed in into a gorgeous woman, always smart, and now a powerful, wealthy director.

As she watched him, she couldn't decide if it would be better to hire him or tell him he simply wasn't right for the movie. Either way, she was determined to get her revenge, after all he had made most of her senior year a miserable one. First, she needed to make sure he really didn't recognize her.

"So how long have you played football, Steve?" she interrupted.

"Started in Peewee League, played quarterback in high school, got a full scholarship to college, and was drafted by the NFL," he bragged.

"Why did you stop?" she asked, smiling at him.

"Well, you know years of playing at the highest levels takes its toll, but I assure you I know the game inside and out and will make sure your actors play their parts well."

She decided then and there he had no idea who she was and offered, "Well, thank you for coming, we have a few more interviews, but we'll be in touch in a few days with our decision."

Steve wanted the last word, "Thank you ma'am." He stood, "Rick, I hope to hear from you. I know I can do a good job for you both."

After her abrupt dismissal, Rick looked at her quizzically, "What gives?"

"I just knew we had several more people to see. I'm hoping we can make a decision on these consultants today. What did you think of him?" she covered.

"It seems like he knows football, but I'm not sure what else." Rick laughed.

"Agreed," Anne replied, "but that's all we need, right?"

They spent the rest of the day interviewing a couple of other "football experts" but Steve, who was new to the consulting game would be the least expensive. Anne and Rick decided to give him a callback.

~~~~~~~~

Steve was somewhat confused by the way the meeting had gone. Rick had seemed friendly enough and engaged, but the director was, well, he couldn't figure her out. She was gorgeous for sure, but seemed all business, not at all the type of woman to whom he was normally attracted. Still, Steve was intrigued. She reminded him of someone, but he couldn't figure out who. After two wives and a number of female conquests along the way, it could be anyone.

Wife number one he had met during his college career. He was the team's quarterback and she was a leader on the cheer squad. They married as soon as he was drafted. It didn't last long, the professional football life left them both with too much free time and too many distractions. He took a lover and when she found out, she did as well. They only lasted two years.

Shortly after the divorce, he had found another beauty who turned out to be more attracted to his celebrity and money than to him. It lasted less than a year.

Steve had been relatively single since then, a fact not helped by the end of his NFL career. An old college buddy had hooked him up with his first consulting gig on a short-lived sitcom. Next, he found himself consulting on a teenage B-movie, and later another job on a TV show. He was making a name for himself, but his niche was small, so he hoped he had made a positive impression. He felt he had done well with Rick, the producer, but Anne, the director, seemed another story. He longed for another opportunity to impress her, in more ways than one.

A few days later, when the call came, he was genuinely surprised. The director had called herself offering him the position as a consultant on the movie. He quickly accepted, thrilled he had made a better impression than he had imagined.

~~~~~~~~~

Everyone had worked hard the weeks leading up to filming. Anne and Rick had numerous meetings. She had even met with Steve several times to finalize some details and make some changes to the script to ensure authenticity to the football-laden actions scenes.

Their first meeting had been very professional. They talked about the first scenes to be shot and some minor changes which were needed to remain true to the game. They scheduled a second meeting in her office, to continue their review. Just before the meeting, Steve called to ask if she could meet him at a favorite coffee shop rather than her office.

She agreed to meet him and thought, *"So the game begins."*

The coffee shop consultation went well. Steve continued to try to charm her, but she kept it strictly business. She honestly wanted to see how far he would go.

The next time they planned to meet, he asked if they could do it over lunch. She agreed. Again, Steve tried to find out more about her, but she provided little. He shared about his football career and how he got into the consulting business. She told him she had two fine arts degrees. It was all he learned.

Before their next meeting, Steve tried to find out more about Anne, but it was difficult. Obviously she kept a tight hand on her personal information. Someone indicated she had been married at least once, but he couldn't find out any details. Even when he asked others who were connected to the film, he found out very little.

Over the coming weeks, they met more often, discussing changes to the script. They saw each other often on the set. He discovered, quite accidentally, Trey Davidson, a mediocre actor who played mostly supporting roles was her ex. He had stopped by her office for a meeting just as Trey stormed out, "You could have helped me get the part, Annie, you owe me that much!" and slammed the door.

She was expecting him so he knocked, and she said simply, "Come in" as if nothing out of the ordinary had happened.

"Are you okay? What was that all about?" He looked truly concerned.

Anne knew better. "Oh…that was about Trey…surely you understand, having been married before?" she questioned.

Steve nodded, "Yes." It was the first really personal information she had shared, but she didn't offer more and he didn't ask. He knew she was smart and savvy or she wouldn't have gotten this far in the tough industry that was film-making. It made him want her all the more.

Steve felt as if he was getting to know Anne better, but Anne continued to play the game, letting him believe she was opening up, much as he had done to her years ago. She hadn't decided what the end game would be, but the more she was around him, the more she wanted revenge for the scars he had inflicted on her. It was true, they had been exacerbated by Trey's equally unique betrayal, but she had already taken care of him as his career, which he cared about more than anything, was slowly going down the toilet.

Once she had her revenge on Steve, she knew she could get on with her life and her career.

Steve continued his pursuit, never realizing his quarry was actually the predator.

Steve finally thought he was making progress with Anne the night she agreed to dinner with him without script in hand. He was taking her to Chateau Marmont and hoping to impress. *"Maybe tonight will be the night,"* he thought.

They had a lovely and delectable dinner, among the rich and famous, many who paid accolades to Anne on her most recent success or wished her the best for the current film, the story of an NFL star whose extracurricular amorous activities had gotten him shot by a jealous lover leading to a complex, yet fun whodunnit. She introduced him to everyone, as if she was delighted to have him on her arm for the evening.

As the night went on, he slipped his arm around her and she delicately stroked his hand. *"Finally, I am getting somewhere,"* he reasoned. *"Maybe tonight I'll even get an invite for a nightcap."*

Steve escorted Anne home. At the door, as she thanked him for a lovely dinner and lingered, he leaned in for a kiss, but she quickly turned so it landed on cheek. She touched his hand, "Remember, we've got an early call for the final scenes tomorrow?" and disappeared into the house.

The following morning, Rick, Anne, and Steve were on set early, advising some of the actors and making sure the scene was blocked properly for the final shots of the film. The process had been long but it had all gone well and everything seemed to indicate another blockbuster.

Steve was busy patting himself on the back. Though it had taken some time, Anne would soon be his latest conquest. Yet it was so much more. Never before had he had to try so hard to win a woman's affections but Anne was different. She was as smart as she was sexy. It wasn't hard for him to imagine her as wife number three. His thoughts betrayed him as he wondered, *"Is this the real thing? Have I fallen for Anne? It is certainly different than any of my relationships in the past. Except maybe for that super shy girl way back in high school...she had been different, but he had blown it and there was no going back. Wonder where she is today?*

Anne, in full-on director-mode interrupted his thoughts, "Is everyone ready Steve? Have you made the changes we discussed? We really need these final scenes to bring it all together."

"Yes, ma'am," he answered, knowing she would accept no disrespect on the set.

"Let's run through it once more before the final take," she winked so only he could see.

He was stunned. He had never seen her do anything like that, *"I've got her now,"* he smiled.

The final scene was the murder of the NFL superstar by one of his lovers in the middle of practice. He brought one of his current lovers to watch his practice session not knowing she had discovered his infidelities the night before. He failed to remember he had also provide passes for a few other paramours, past, present, and even future, so when shots rang out, the mystery of whodunnit began in earnest.

Everyone found their places for the practice run through, Steve squarely in the middle of it all, obviously enjoying his new level of celebrity and his anticipated celebratory seduction of Anne once the filming was wrapped today.

The scene was set. Steve was giving final instructions to the actor playing the NFL star when Anne called out, "Action." As expected, the shots rang out, the actor, looked stunned and fell to the ground as the other players dropped to the ground or ran for cover.

Anne called, "Cut" as everyone got up to return to their positions for the final take. Steve did not move.

Anne jumped from her chair and ran to his side, screaming "Steve's been shot, someone call 911."

Before the studio medics could arrive, Anne leaned in to kiss Steve, "Thank you for making me the woman I am today, *En un beso, sabrás todo lo que he callado.*[2]"

His eyes flicker open a final time, questioning, as recognition dawns. His mind whispers, *"Kelly ANNE Stowe"* but the words won't come.

"Yes," Anne says, "Shhhh...."

Emergency services arrived as Steve breathed his last, her kiss of revenge only visible by the bold Stila Fia *Beso* Lipstick she wore.

---

[2] In a kiss, you will know everything that I have kept quiet.

A PROFITABLE KISS

2021-2022

January 2021

On the first workday of the New Year, the employees of MacLeod Enterprises were bustling excitedly. After unexpected and extremely generous year-end bonuses for those in the C-suite, corporate gossip buzzed – the company was poised perfectly for its biggest year yet.

Having only been with the company for a few years, Karen Spencer wanted a piece of the proverbial pie. She was smart and attractive, but had yet to gain much traction moving up the corporate ladder. She had been working hard, but her superiors didn't seem to notice. Her sales numbers were good, and though not the best, they were better than most. She simply couldn't understand why she wasn't gaining ground like some of her male counterparts. She had pondered the issue over the holidays, particularly after she heard about the big year-end bonuses received by those individuals in upper management.

After thoughtful consideration, Karen developed a new plan. Her New Year's resolution was about to change it all. It was time for her to get ahead and 2021 was going to be her year – one way or another. She'd been working hard, taking on extra tasks to gain experience, but without the desired results.

As 2021 began, she launched her plan, a fast track scheme which if played well would land her a seat on the board of directors at MacLeod Enterprises in record time. She knew she would have to be careful and handle every interaction and transaction with precision, but she felt her plan could not fail.

Her first step involved a complete makeover – hair, makeup, and wardrobe. Every aspect of her new corporate image needed to scream professional but be carefully coupled with a healthy underlying measure of unabashed sex appeal. She was done with all the hard work. She would rise to the top using her brains and her body to get where she wanted – a seat on the board – when she wanted – by the end of 2022.

Karen Spencer strolled into the MacLeod building, head held high. For the first day of the rest of her life, she had chosen a form-fitting black business suit with black leather spool heeled pumps. Underneath, should anyone decide to sneak a peek, she had chosen a corset top and lace trimmed cheeky panties. The lingerie was black with hints of gold, a little hint of perfect glimmer for catching the eye of her prey should the opportunity arise.

She had only used this technique once before – to land the job at MacLeod. That time, she had found herself at a networking event in the city. It was a cocktail party in which those in the market for a job could mingle with lower level executives and make connections. Karen had gone with a former co-worker, Lisa Brown, and the two women were soon approached by Phil Davis and Henry Vick of MacLeod Enterprises. Karen and Lisa knew a little about the company which predominantly handled pharmaceutical sales for a number of big pharma entities and dabbled in a variety of sales in other areas.

At the time, Karen had some minor sales experience and was interested as her current position held little opportunity for the future. She wanted more, so she flirted a bit. Phil took her aside under the guise of getting her Cosmopolitan refilled and talking about a potential sales job in the MacLeod pharmaceutical sales division. She was intrigued, so she went along with him just to see what he had to say.

As the conversation continued along with the drink refills, she was more fascinated by the position Phil described, particularly its salary potential. She tried to make what little sales experience she had sound better, but Phil wasn't convinced, yet. She continued her efforts with a different approach. She leaned in, touched his arm, and began her seduction. She couldn't care less about Phil, but she really wanted the job and she knew a surefire way to get it. While she hadn't tried it before, she knew a couple of people, male and female, who had done it successfully, so why shouldn't she?

She ordered another round of drinks and continued to flirt with Phil. She complained about the heat in the room and slipped off her suit jacket to reveal a filmy silk blouse which left little to the imagination. Having had just enough to drink, Phil was quickly on the hook. She

continued her play, and soon Phil invited her to join him at

his downtown condo for another drink while they discussed

the position at MacLeod. She agreed and the rest was

history.

Phil believed he had seduced her, not the other way

around, and she secured the job with a few thinly veiled

threats. She started her job at MacLeod the following week

when she entered the pharmaceutical sales training

program. She hadn't seen Phil again, but heard he'd gone to

another division of the company shortly after their

rendezvous.

From that point on, up until now, Karen had worked

hard hoping to climb to the top with her intelligence and

work ethic. In her mind, her perception was misguided,

believing in only three short years in such a competitive

industry would yield a meteoric rise. For most, a seat at the table only came after 10, 15, or even 20 years of hard work and ongoing achievements. Karen had no intention of waiting so long, she was done with all that, planning to take an alternate and considerably quicker route.

Karen's first target was her immediate supervisor, Carlton O'Hara. Carl had been with the company longer than her, but seemed to be content in his district supervisor position. He had one of the best sales teams in the company which earned him considerable commissions and seemed to make him happy. He was married with two kids, one already in college, the second leaving in the fall. Maybe Carl was stuck or maybe the job was enough for him. Not so for Karen. She wanted more, much more. And she was tired of waiting.

She stepped into Carl's office and asked, "Carl, like me, you've been with MacLeod for some time. I've been working hard, but I'm really hoping you can give me some tips on taking the next step into a supervisory role. How did you do it?"

Carl was no stranger to this type of request, even so, he noticed something different about Karen, and stared a little too long before answering.

"Carl? Is everything okay?" she interrupted his thoughts.

"Yes, Karen, fine. So you want to make your move up the ladder?"

"I do." Karen offered, crossing her legs seductively, "And I'm hoping you can help."

"It's really not a good time, I have back to back meetings today, could we meet tomorrow?"

Unknowingly, he was playing right into her hand, "How about dinner after I finish my route? That way, we'll be off the clock and it won't affect your busy schedule."

Carl glanced at his smartphone's calendar, "Not today, but how about Wednesday? I'll pull your latest sales numbers in the meantime, and see what I can do to help."

"Perfect." Karen stood, leaning in, giving him a quick glance at her décolletage and lace corset. "Thank you so much Carl."

He cleared his throat and answered, "You're welcome" while his mind wondered, *has she always looked so good?*

****

Wednesday arrived, and Karen asked Carl if he knew Amato's, a little Italian café downtown. He told her he'd heard of it but had never been. She crooned, "They have the best cannoli. It's near my last sales call today, could we meet there around seven?"

He agreed again thinking to himself, *there is something different about her.* He knew better than to comment on her appearance in the office, less it be

misconstrued as some sort of sexual harassment, but *damn*,

he thought, *she gets more sensual by the day.*

They met after work at Amato's, ordered drinks,

and were soon deep in discussion, with Carl giving Karen

advice on how to move forward with her career, "Your

sales numbers are good and I see you've taken several

additional routes. All good, and each encounter gives you

more experience in the business."

"Thanks Carl, but honestly, I want more. After three

years, I'd like to work my way up – maybe to a position

like yours next and then start working on the next level,"

she paused, "It's warm in here isn't it?" She casually

slipped off her blazer to reveal a form fitting bodycon top,

conservatively cut, but highlighting every curve.

Carl listened, but was finding it difficult to focus.

She was twenty years his junior, what was he thinking? He

found his voice, "There is no reason you shouldn't be able to go to the top, if you keep up the hard work."

She pouted just enough, "It just seems I'm stuck, when I want so much more, what would you recommend?"

The waitress interrupted, and they ordered dinner and more drinks. Carl continued to offer industry tips and ways Karen could make herself more valuable to the company as they enjoyed their meal. Karen continued to ask questions, kept the topic on business, and flattered Carl at every opportunity.

After the promised "best cannoli in town," and as they were leaving, she clumsily bumped the table sending the leftovers into Carl's lap. She quickly apologized, reaching for a napkin to wipe away the sauce from his lap, only to discover exactly what she expected. Carl was ready for seduction.

"I'm so sorry, Carl," she continued, "My apartment is just a few blocks away, why don't you come with me and let me help you get cleaned up before you head home? It'll only take a few minutes and you can be on your way."

He hesitated before agreeing to her invitation, "You really think you can get the stain out quickly?"

"Yes, of course, I know just the trick," she offered as he got up and followed her out the door.

They arrived at her apartment in short order and she promptly told Carl, "Take off your pants and let me get the club soda. I'll grab you a robe to slip on while I get the stain out."

She spoke so matter-of-factly, Carl obeyed, as she headed into the other room, quickly returning with the promised robe. She smiled sweetly, "Would you like something to drink while you wait?"

He agreed and once more she disappeared. This time, her return was not so circumspect. She had changed into what appeared to Carl to be a nightdress or maybe a slip and presented him with his drink.

He stared for a moment, unsure of what was happening.

Karen noted his rising manhood and it was all the invitation she needed.

****

Carl performed as expected and hastily acquiesced to Karen's "request" for promotion. She didn't like to call it "blackmail" but rather "mutually beneficial support." Within a month of the "Carl encounter," Karen was offered a district supervisor position. She was now Carl's equal.

She learned her new role rapidly, and continued with her scheme, quickly setting her sights on her next goal.

****

2021 Continued

Throughout 2021, Karen "worked" her way up the corporate ladder. Her path was unconventional but it was going as planned and didn't require all the work she had previously put in while she was under Carl's leadership in her early sales position.

She continued her pattern of conquest in her climb upward, seducing her way to middle management on the backs of "business" meetings which led to blackmail of her male colleagues. She wasn't above using her methods to increase her divisions sales numbers to help her cause, sleeping with her biggest clients and then demanding their "mutually beneficial support" as she deemed it. They simply called it blackmail.

After landing successfully, though suspiciously, in her middle management position, Karen used sedition or seduction to compromise her middle management colleagues standing at MacLeod Enterprises and move past them toward upper management.

****

2022

As 2022 dawned, Karen could see her path toward a seat on the board more clearly, but the process was moving too slowly. She knew she needed bigger marks, players higher up the ladder. By the end of the second quarter, Karen was still blackmailing, seducing, and bribing anyone in the company who could give her an edge or nudge the door open a little further. She had added to her list of targets multimillion dollar clients, who as they were brought into the MacLeod fold had begun to get her noticed by the Board of Directors. As she saw it, she only needed one more large acquisition and then should find herself up for a seat on the board of directors.

She had the new client in her sights – a national affiliation of physicians with offices all over the country and specialists in every field of medicine. The group had started the practice in New York City only 10 years prior and now has expanded its reach across the country. In recent months, the word on the street, was they were shopping for a new distributor that could handle their extensive and growing volume of pharmaceutical needs.

Karen knew exactly how to play it and the upcoming national pharmaceutical convention in Atlanta, GA, would provide the opening she needed. She arrived, in style, with several other high-ranking members of the MacLeod team. MacLeod was one of the largest sponsors of the event and they also had a large exhibition area at the convention which gave her entrée into every event, even the exclusive President's Gala. She was also scheduled to speak alongside her colleagues as part of the training and education sessions. She had all the access she needed to work her "magic." She had planned her wardrobe carefully, as she always did, with the perfect blend of business savvy and sensuality. Equally stacked was her itinerary ensuring access to her unsuspecting marks throughout the convention.

Karen quickly went to work, confident this weekend's exploits would seal her seat on the board. She had done her research. From her latest mark, she knew which doctors would be in play – Dr. Andrew Bray, Dr. Clark Morrison, and Dr. Teresa Larson – all board members of the national physician's practice. She had targeted Dr. Bray as the easiest mark of the three. His marriage had just enough struggles, but his finances were boundless as one of the company's founders. If it didn't work out with Dr. Bray, then Dr. Morrison was next. If they both failed to meet her expectations, she knew she could just as easily seduce Dr. Larson.

At the meet and greet, a cocktail party, Karen donned one of her favorite little black dresses a bodycon number with a seemingly judicious neckline, and a daring, plunging back, thoughtfully hidden with a lace inlaid wrap, until needed. She quickly found herself caught up in the introductions with Dr. Bray, Dr. Morrison, and Dr. Larson. They shared drinks and small talk for a few minutes as Karen carefully assessed the three doctors for their potential to help her plan succeed.

It didn't take long for Dr. Bray and Dr. Larson to excuse themselves to greet others, but Dr. Morrison lingered. Little did he know, he now had a target on his back. He offered to get her another drink, returning quickly with his own refilled as well.

After a bit more conversation and securing an appointment for tomorrow, Karen offered, "Thanks for the drink Dr. Morrison, I look forward to meeting with you and *your team* tomorrow." She knew a little flattery which made him sound like the leader couldn't hurt her cause.

"Thank you Karen, and please, you must call me Clark."

"Of course, Dr....I mean...Clark. I'll look forward to seeing your tomorrow," she spoke softly as she turned away. Sitting her empty glass on a nearby table, she let her wrap fall, just enough, to the curve of back.

"Let me help you with that..." Clark to the rescue said as he lifted the wrap, a little too slowly, back up to her shoulders.

"Thank you," she breathed. "See you tomorrow," she continued, as she shot him her most seductive smile and walked slowly away.

The following morning, Karen was ready in the conference room, garbed in her favorite form-fitting black business suit and black patent leather high heeled pumps, awaiting the arrival of the three doctors. Beneath her suit, and true to form, she chose a push-up corset with just the right amount of bling and matching bikini panties in case the opportunity arose.

She was all business as the doctors arrived, ready with her presentation and pitch for MacLeod to supply all the burgeoning practice's needs. Karen was ready with the answers to all their questions, continually reassuring them of MacLeod's ability to provide all their pharmaceuticals, on time, every time, and at the right price.

Drs. Bray, Morrison, and Larson thanked her for her presentation, but confessed they had two more to hear before the education sessions began in the afternoon.

Karen asked, "I'd like the opportunity to meet with you all once more before you make your final decision. I'm sure MacLeod can meet or beat any offer.

They agreed, in unison, to meet with her once on the last day of the conference. To Karen, it seemed a positive sign, they all appeared to like her straightforward, business approach. She was pleased with her progress thus far and inquired, "Might I take you all to lunch today?"

Dr. Bray answered for the group, "We already have a lunch meeting today, but perhaps tomorrow?"

"Yes, of course, how about one?"

They readily agreed. Karen took the opportunity to invite them to hear her training session. Drs. Bray and Larson admitted to having another session on their schedule, but Dr. Morrison promised to attend. As they exited the conference room, she thanked them all with a handshake, lingering a few seconds longer with Clark's hand and then touching his shoulder as he walked away.

Later that afternoon, as promised, Dr. Clark Morrison attended Karen's educational session. She was dressed as she had been for their earlier meeting, at which he could have sworn he glimpsed only a bra or corset under her suit jacket, no blouse at all. Clark looked and listened to Karen's talk, wondering again about her business attire. He was impressed at her knowledge of the industry.

In truth, Clark was the youngest member of the entourage, but with the acquisition of his wife, who was the daughter of one of the founding partners, he had become an equal partner in the business. He knew he still had a lot to prove to the other partners who had joined the business in more traditional ways. He also realized he needed to control his roving eye, even so there was something about Karen Spencer, a rising star at MacLeod. If he had his way, they would have signed an exclusive contract with her earlier and skipped the other presentations, but he could wait.

Karen noted Clark's arrival and glanced at him periodically during her presentation. After she was done, she saw him lingering at the back of those offering their accolades and asking her questions about the latest advancements in the industry.

"Dr…I mean…Clark, thanks for coming. What did you think?" Karen asked.

"Great job, very knowledgeable, particularly of all that is in the pipeline."

"Did you have any questions? Comments? I'd love a bit of free feedback." She pressed.

"Well, sure, but how about we grab a drink first?" He offered, unable to stop himself.

"Are you sure? I know you have a lot on your plate." Karen countered, not wanting to sound overly interested.

"Absolutely, if you have time, of course?" He replied.

"Yes, I do. I'm actually done for today, until tonight's dinner." She smiled. She had him, all she had to do was perform her work as she always did and she'd have the contract and her seat at the table.

She tested the waters, "Would you like to get out of here for a while? I know a great little bar not too far from here."

"Sure, why not? Let's go."

They walked toward the bar, chatting casually before arriving at the trendy little bistro she had mentioned.

They ordered drinks, today's feature, and over the first drink kept the conversation on the business of medication. By the second drink, the conversation turned more personal. Karen didn't even try very hard to capture his attention, he obviously already had her on his radar as he flirted shamelessly. She leaned in, giving him a quick glimpse of her rhinestone embellished corset which also showed off the tops of her rounded, ample breasts. She grinned, this was going to be a fun one! Young Dr. Clark Morrison was hot, toned, and from all appearances ready to bed her, but she didn't want to make it too easy, "Oh look at the time," she declared, "I've got to get back and get changed for tonight. I'm doing the speaker introductions at the dinner."

"Yes," he reluctantly agreed, "I guess we should get back."

They walked back quietly, contemplating what might come next. It wasn't all that unusual to anticipate the unexpected, no strings attached hook-ups at these sort of events, but he was surprised they had connected so quickly.

Back at the hotel and convention center, each headed for their rooms, leaving their options open.

Karen donned a black one shoulder maxi dress, streamlined design with a side slit way up to there and gold strappy heels. Beneath she had chosen a gold minimalist bra with matching thong, planning her night of seduction for young, hot Dr. Morrison. She knew his story all too well. He had come into the practice on the heels of his marriage to the daughter of one of the founding partners. There was little doubt an affair would have devastating effects on his career and his newfound wealth. The game was afoot!

At the dinner, Karen introduced the keynote speaker with her usual charisma and then took her seat among her colleagues who included Carmen Winn, Dr. James Jay, and the MacLeods, Jessica (chairwoman) and Michael (president). She had hoped their son Liam (board member) would be in attendance, but as usual he was nowhere to be found. She knew she needed to make a connection with him sooner rather than later as he was part of her master plan, but that would have to wait for another time.

After the dinner concluded, the bar was open and convention attendees mingled at will. She approached Dr. Bray, "I trust you are having a productive trip, Dr. Bray."

He answered, eyeing her warily, "Yes, so far so good." He had recognized her type immediately, her goal was the top, and she would use anything or anyone to get there. Even so, he realized, she might be the best fit as their suppliers because of MacLeod's incredible connections, and added, "I'm looking forward to our meeting tomorrow."

"Yes, I am too."

"Please excuse me, I need to speak to Dr..." and his voice trailed off as he moved quickly away.

"I see Andrew gave you his usual brush off..." Clark approached from behind.

She nodded, turning, "Yes, it would seem so, but I'm sure I have the best offer you've heard."

"Don't be so sure, your competitors offered some strong incentives," he grinned.

"Oh really," she flirted, playing the game.

"Yes, but I might add, none of them look as fetching as you, Ms. Spencer."

"Thank you, Dr. Morrison, you clean up quite nicely yourself," She revealed, looking him up and down slowly, seductively moistening her lips.

They were engaged in the dance, but for the curious, it was difficult to determine who was being seduced.

"Looks like you need another drink," Clark whispered, "I'll grab two and meet you on the terrace."

"Why Dr. Morrison, what are you suggesting?" She laughed, slowly moving toward the aforementioned terrace.

Moments later they met under the moonlight on the deserted terrace. Karen hadn't expected it to be empty, but she was pleased.

Unknown to either of them, Dr. Larson, one of the curious, had watched the exchange. As one of the company founders, she considered Clark's wife and in-laws as family, and she wanted to know more. She had positioned herself in the shadows, not close enough to hear, but certainly near enough to see.

At first, Karen and Clark appeared as colleagues, simply chatting over drinks, while they sat at a small table. Karen crossed her legs, allowing Clark a glimpse of her shapely thigh all the way up to the sensual curve of her well-rounded derriere. His admiration was evident, as he leaned closer, whispered in her ear, and gently laid a hand on her thigh. The feel was undeniably electric.

Dr. Larson, still silently watching, heard herself being paged. She was frustrated, but knew she must answer the call and so slipped away unnoticed by the pair.

Karen, always on the alert, thought she heard someone moving on the terrace. *Were they being watched? Well, that would definitely not do.* She casually moved Clark's hand, crooning, "I felt it too, but not here. Neither of us can afford to have our reputations compromised."

Damn, she was right, he thought, *but there was no denying he wanted her and now.* He uttered the words, "You're right" but they both remained unmoved as the moments passed. It only increased his desire.

She looked around, ensuring no one was near, and leaned forward, gently caressing his thigh, "We could take this up to my suite, if you'd like?" she hummed as she caught hold of his powerful member.

He nodded. She slipped him keycard as they feigned goodnights and went their separate ways.

Moments later, he entered her suite to see her standing in front of the open window, still in that sexy off the shoulder dress. He caught his breath, had a fleeting thought of his wife, and stepped toward her as she let her dress fall to the floor. He couldn't stop the tide now if he tried. She had him. To seal the deal, she kissed him as he tugged and twisted out of his clothes.

****

Dr. Clark Morrison succumbed to Karen's charms, realizing too late that he was truly sunk. As he exited her room in the wee hours of the morning, the deal had been struck, he would agree to her contract and convince the others to do so as well, or she would share with his bride and well-established father-in-law how he had spent the

night. And well, yes, Karen had the proof, just like she

always did.

Hours later, the meeting went exactly as Karen had

planned. Though there was slight pushback from Dr.

Larson, it seemed Dr. Bray was easily on board. Karen had

secured her latest multi-million dollar client, could a seat

on the board be far behind?

****

Karen was offered a seat on the board shortly after

the acquisition, but she still wanted more. She wanted the

president's job, but that would be no easy task given who

the president was – none other than Michael MacLeod

himself. Even still, she believed there was no reason she

couldn't get there, knowing she could easily sleep her way

to the top and complete control.

What she failed to realize was the board consisted of a well-rounded mix of individuals, whose age, experience, and talent spoke for themselves. Everyone on the board had seen her type before, but they couldn't deny her success. Some had a number of suspicions, none of which they could prove, so they had quietly and carefully watched the rise of Karen Spencer, ultimately offering her the seat on the board, which by all appearances she had earned.

****

Mid-year 2022

Soon after accepting her seat on the board, the company president, Michael MacLeod, announced his retirement. The reason was all quite hush-hush but the rumor mill was hard at work doling out stories of a variety of medical concerns.

As others expressed sadness because MacLeod was a visionary leader who had led his company to ever increasing heights, Karen saw yet another opportunity in Liam MacLeod, MacLeod Enterprises heir apparent. Liam, son of President MacLeod and his wife Jessica MacLeod, chairwoman of the company, sat on the board, though he was not directly involved in the company.

Having heard the rumors about his father, Karen approached Liam at the end of third quarter board meeting, "I'm sorry to hear about your father, he is such a great leader, he will be missed." Even as she spoke, she wondered, *"Has he always looked this good? I know it's been months since I've seen him, but damn, he's fine!"*

"Thank you Karen, yes, I'm sure he will," Liam responded.

"I was also saddened by the news of his ill health," she continued. She hoped she wasn't staring, *he's obviously done something different, even in his suit, his body looks*

hard, chiseled even.

"What do you mean?"

Karen confessed, "I've only heard rumors, but I have been in business long enough to know there is always some truth behind them."

Pulling her aside, Liam spoke softly, his voice stiff, "There is some truth, but you are the first person to have the courage to speak to me about it."

"I didn't mean to overstep," she began, "I just hope you know I am sorry to hear it, but I would be happy to listen if you ever want to talk."

Liam smiled. "Thank you," he added, walking away.

Karen didn't like being dismissed, but she let it go for the moment, willing to give it a few days before reaching out to him again. She watched him leave, there was definitely something different. She knew he'd never looked so good. He carried himself with a confidence he hadn't had before. It was evident in the air about him, but even more in his physicality. He had been part of her master plan all along but after seeing him today, she knew she'd like to make it personal but if needed, she'd keep it all business. All she needed was an in, and she never seemed to have any difficulty finding one.

A week later, she got her break. She had been working, late for her, and there he was, Liam MacLeod, exiting the building with almost perfect timing. *Damn, he looks good.* She knew in an instant he was going to be excellent in bed, she just had to get him there. At that moment, he was staring at his phone, oblivious to her presence.

He must have been meeting with his father, she thought as she hastened her step and bumped into him pretending not to have seen him. *Yes, hard body, yes, ripped, yes, the coming conquest would be worthwhile…*

"Liam," she said, "What a nice surprise!"

"Hello Karen, working late?" he inquired.

"Yes, sometimes I do my best work when it's quiet and everyone has gone for the day," she lied. *She rarely worked late, she didn't really have to, after all, she had a number of individuals on whom she could call for "mutually beneficial support."*

Turning her attention back to Liam, "What brings you here?"

He countered, "A quick meeting with my dad," responding hastily to change the subject, "Have you had dinner?"

"No, I haven't."

"Why don't we grab a late supper, that is, if you don't have other plans?" he queried.

"I'd love too," came her almost too quick reply. *Calm down,* she told herself, *this is the chance you've been waiting for!*

"Great! There's a new Thai restaurant not far from here, The Lotus something or other, let's grab a cab."

Karen couldn't believe her luck. It was as if Liam had literally fallen right into her lap. She had to remind herself to stay composed and keep the dinner as business-like as possible. Only then could she get a read on Liam regarding business, the board, and any other useful information she could glean from dinner and casual conversation.

The food was delicious and dinner with Liam was pleasant and comfortable. She was a bit surprised, having always heard he was essentially a spoiled rich kid. In fact, Liam was genuinely concerned about his father's health concerns. He also shared how he hoped to develop a new philanthropic foundation for MacLeod Enterprises.

She was actually interested in hearing what he had to say, a reaction she hadn't had in a long time with anyone. She had to remind herself of the endgame, to get the needed votes to become the new president of the board on Michael MacLeod's retirement. She knew she was close but if she could get Liam on her side, she'd have the clout and votes to pull it off.

****

Over the next month, she found herself drawn to Liam, and he seemed to be interested in her as well. She had toned down the sensuality at first, hoping to lure him in with her business knowledge. As she felt more comfortable playing him, she decided to turn up the heat, once again donning her sultry business attire, tailored black suit, with little underneath, and high heels. On the nights they met for drinks, she opted out of her business suit and often wore one of her favorite little black dresses just to up the ante.

As they spent more and more time together, she felt a greater ease. One evening they attended an art gallery opening. She chose stilettos, paired with a halter mini dress which left little to the imagination. The evening went according to plan with an abundance of sensual innuendo but ended abruptly when he took a call from his father. He kissed her passionately, whispered, "Next time…"

A week later, determined to bed him (and close the deal), she invited him for a later supper at her home. It as a bold move and she was surprised when he countered with an intimate dinner in the rooftop restaurant of his building. She acquiesced, his place would be even better than hers. She chose her outfit carefully, opting for a sheer barely-there black dress with a double breasted low cut suit jacket. Dinner was exquisite as was the dancing afterward.

Dancing was always incredibly sexy with Liam whose fit, hot body made him the perfect partner.

As she strategized how to invite herself back to his place, he suggested, "One more dance and back to my place for a drink, beautiful?

She demurred, "That sounds perfect…"

Their final dance was a slow one, giving her the opportunity to press in close and begin the foreplay. She stroked his passion. He caressed her with equal desire. It was as if they were alone on a private dance floor.

The music stopped, and reluctantly they returned to the table, continuing the flirtation. As Liam took care of the check, she excused herself to freshen up.

When she returned, she was livid to see him once again on the phone. He turned to her, his face downtrodden, "It was my mother, she is headed to the hospital with my father. I have to go."

She turned her anger quickly to concern and sweetly offered to accompany him.

He declined, "No, it's late, and there's really nothing to do but go and wait. I'll have the car brought round for you and I'll grab an uber. I'm sorry, my love." He pulled her close and held her, kissing her with obvious desire, "I'll make it up to you soon."

There it was! She had him. He hadn't exactly professed his love, but he was close, and she hadn't even bedded him!

The car was waiting outside when they arrived in the lobby. He walked her out and settled her in, kissing her once more. She looked back to see him wave as the driver headed to her condo.

Moments later, Liam headed back inside.

On the way home, Karen was confident, certain she had him all wrapped up. She just needed to close the deal.

Liam called her the following day to report his father was fine, just dehydrated.

Karen and Liam carried on, enjoying one another's company, going to all the best places for dinner and drinks, discussing topics like her meteoric rise in the company and his plans for the future of the MacLeod Foundation.

Neither had made another overture, then it happened. One night, after a lovely dinner and a stroll in the park, they sat on a park bench admiring the starlit night. As he moved his arm around her, Karen seized the moment and kissed him sultrily, under the moonlight. It would, she hoped, be a most profitable kiss. He returned the kiss, and remarked, "It's getting late, maybe I should get you home, after all we have a big day tomorrow."

She paused, looking into his eyes, "Maybe…or…better yet…you could join me for a nightcap?

He looked at her thoughtfully, "I don't know Karen, the timing may be just a bit off, what with the board meeting tomorrow and everything. We need to be careful, to ensure everything goes as planned."

She nodded. She had him. She just knew it.

****

What she didn't know was the MacLeod board had been watching, keeping close tabs on the budding relationship between her and Liam. Even now, she and Liam were being watched, as they had been nearly every night since their happenstance meeting at the office and their impromptu Thai dinner.

****

Liam dropped Karen off at her luxury apartment with a single kiss before saying goodnight. As she entered her home, she considered the possibilities. She had been working this angle for two long years. She wanted the President's job. The board would vote tomorrow.

The position was hers. She knew it. She felt it. Her dream was about to come true. She had bribed, seduced, and blackmailed plenty of people to get to this moment. She believed she had enough backing to win the vote and become president of the company, leaving all the other board members behind.

It would be close, but with Liam on her side, she could even eliminate the threat from the quiet and confident Carmen Winn, the extremely talented, savvy, and successful member of the board who was everyone's favorite choice. Winn was 60 years old and had spent the last 20-plus years working her way to the top.

Karen pondered the competition, then laughed, "What competition?" She had sealed the deal with a kiss and she didn't even use her bed this time, She felt confident that Liam would back her bid for President.

****

She arrived at the office early, hoping to have a few moments with Liam before the board convened. On her way in, she caught a glimpse of Phil Davis and Carlton O'Hara, who both still worked for the company, and a few others of whom she had taken advantage to get to this point. She greeted them as she often did, as though they had real working relationships and weren't being held captive under her thumb.

Liam arrived with only a few minutes to spare and spoke to her briefly. To Karen, it seemed he was still attempting to keep up appearances, but as soon as she was named President, she was sure he would acknowledge their relationship before the board and the entire company.

At 10 a.m. the board was gathered, ready to elect the new president of MacLeod Enterprises. Michael MacLeod was not in attendance as he was currently in home care, supposedly recovering from some mysterious treatment. The corporate lawyer would handle the board meeting with him.

The tension in the room was obvious, thought the staff had attempted to create a welcoming atmosphere with a specialty coffee bar and delectable brunch items for the board members to enjoy.

As the meeting was called to order, complete with roll call, all the board members were present and prepared to vote. Everyone in the room knew the future of the company depended on the outcome of today's vote. The voting would be done by ballot and tallied by the corporate lawyer and his team.

As the votes were cast and tallied, Karen smiled confidently. Within minutes, the corporate secretary entered and announced Mrs. MacLeod's arrival.

Karen's smile faded fast as Chairwoman Jessica MacLeod, a strong regal woman exuding confidence, greeted the board. Karen sat shocked, befuddled, and nervous, as she attempted to catch Liam's attention.

All eyes, including Liam's, were focused on his mother, the chairwoman. She began, "Michael and I began this company many years ago and have successfully grown it into the powerhouse it is today. Our success came through hours of hard work, not only ours, but those of our dedicated, hard-working employees including many of you who have helped grow this company and in doing so guaranteed its future success..."

Karen fidgeted awkwardly. Liam hadn't looked her way, even once, since his mother began her speech.

Mrs. MacLeod continued, "…at MacLeod enterprises, we have great plans for the future, with much more success ahead through the outstanding leadership of our new President…Carmen Winn."

Along with Liam, everyone stood and burst into applause, with the exception of Karen Spencer, who sat as white as a ghost and obviously in shock. Her mind screamed, *"What went wrong?! I had all the votes in place to win. Someone betrayed me."* She scanned the room to ascertain who had the balls to betray her as the newly elected President Winn made her way to the front and took her place of honor beside Mrs. MacLeod.

"Thank you Chairwoman MacLeod," she offered, "for this amazing opportunity. MacLeod Enterprises is in a prime position for the future, with a firm foundation built on values, tradition, ethics, and years of hard work by you,

Michael, and most of the members of the board present today."

She nodded to Liam, "Liam, will you join me for just a moment?"

Liam made his way to the front of the boardroom *finally* eyeing Karen thoughtfully, "Congratulations President Winn. With President Winn at the helm, we would also like to announce the company's latest endeavor, a philanthropic endeavor, the MacLeod Foundation."

The applause continued, as President Winn, interrupted, "Many of you will be pleased to know Liam will be joining the company as the head of the new foundation."

Karen was dumbstruck as the entire room looked her way. *"It was Liam. They know. They know,"* she realized all too late. She made a move for the door, only to be blocked by two men in a black suits.

"Just a minute, Ms. Spencer," Mrs. MacLeod intoned, " I would also like to thank Liam for his cooperation with an ongoing FBI investigation into allegations against you. Given the accusations of ethical violations and the FBI investigation into allegations of blackmail, bribery, and other felony state and federal crimes in an attempt to gain control of MacLeod Enterprises, you are hereby terminated from your position."

Karen stood in silence, watching in horror as the FBI agents moved in her direction, placing handcuffs on her.

Liam looked on as they led Karen out of the room, reading her rights as they went.

As she was escorted out of the board room, Karen glanced back to see Liam kiss his mother on the cheek, congratulating her on her astute leadership, just before exiting the board room with President Winn.

In the lobby, Karen Spencer again saw the people she had used to get to the top, her band of "mutual supporters" as she liked to call them. This time, they were the only ones smiling.

****

January 2023 – Epilogue

The arraignment of Karen Spencer was held on January 9, 2023. In attendance in the courtroom were Michael and Jessica MacLeod, Liam MacLeod, Carmen Winn, and the entire board of MacLeod Enterprises. Also present were Phil Davis, Henry Vick, Carlton O'Hara, Dr. Clark Morrison, Dr. Teresa Larson, and a myriad of others who Karen had bribed, extorted, blackmailed, and threatened over the course of her plan.

They all listened with rapt attention as the charges were read, "Count one, blackmail, count two, fraud, count three extortion, count four, extortion, count five…"

Karen stared straight ahead listening to the charges

thinking…*the kisses she shared with Liam were the same*

as every kiss she had bestowed over the past two years

…false, dishonest, artificial…and seemingly not profitable!

Made in the USA
Columbia, SC
22 November 2024

46986429R00163